Naughty-ish

A Holiday HOTTIES novella

L.B. DUNBAR

www.lbdunbar.com

ROMANCE. FOR SEXY SILVER FOX LOVERS.

Copyright © 2023 Laura Dunbar
L.B. Dunbar Writes, Ltd.
https://www.lbdunbar.com/

Cover Design: Elle Maxwell Designs
Editor: Nicole McCurdy/Emerald Edits
Editor: Gemma Brocato
Proofreader: Karen Fischer

Other Books by L.B. Dunbar

Sterling Falls
Sterling Heat
Sterling Brick
Sterling Streak

Parentmoon

Holiday Hotties (Christmas novellas)
Scrooge-ish
Naughty-ish

Road Trips & Romance
Hauling Ashe
Merging Wright
Rhode Trip

Lakeside Cottage
Living at 40
Loving at 40
Learning at 40
Letting Go at 40

The Silver Foxes of Blue Ridge
Silver Brewer
Silver Player
Silver Mayor
Silver Biker

Sexy Silver Fox Collection
After Care
Midlife Crisis
Restored Dreams
Second Chance
Wine&Dine

Collision novellas
Collide
Caught

L.B. DUNBAR

The Sex Education of M.E.

The Heart Collection
Speak from the Heart
Read with your Heart
Look with your Heart
Fight from the Heart
View with your Heart

A Heart Collection Spin-off
The Heart Remembers

BOOKS IN OTHER AUTHOR WORLDS
Smartypants Romance (an imprint of Penny Reid)
Love in Due Time
Love in Deed
Love in a Pickle

The World of True North (an imprint of Sarina Bowen)
Cowboy
Studfinder

THE EARLY YEARS
The Legendary Rock Star Series

Paradise Stories

The Island Duet

Modern Descendants – writing as elda lore

BLURB

With the name Holliday, you'd think I'd be all about the Christmas season. Most years, I am, but this one not so much. Between my ex being a real Scrooge-in-the-backside, re-entering the workforce, wrangling my two children, and evading my eight-year-old's questions about Santa's existence, I'm struggling to believe in the magic myself.

Enter Nick, my next-door neighbor. My very hot, single, fireman neighbor. He's full of the seasonal spirit from hanging my outdoor Christmas lights to playing Santa for the local church breakfast.

Funny thing about Nick, he kind of resembles the man in red, in a younger, sexier, silver fox way, complete with snow in his beard but rather tight abs suggesting cookies are not part of his diet when they are a staple of mine.

Anywho, he's sweet in a rugged sense, and if he were the man making a list and checking it twice, I'd like to be in his naughty column. Because something tells me being a little naughty-ish with Nick from next door might bring me tidings of comfort and restore my joy in this season.

When he discovers I have a seasonal list myself, he's determined to help me accomplish all the to-dos, only falling in love with my next-door neighbor wasn't one of them.

+ + +

From L.B. Dunbar comes another SHE-grump Christmas tale of holiday shenanigans and jingling bells with a sunshine silver fox.

DEDICATION

For other 'moms' who feel the pressure of the holidays.
Even without being that elf on your shelf, I see you.

L.B. DUNBAR

BE YOUTHFUL

Chapter 1

Where is that fucking elf on a shelf doll?

In preparation for the upcoming Christmas holiday, I'd been searching everywhere for that damn creepy imp that sits on a shelf, pretending to monitor my children's behavior in the weeks before the holiday.

Naughty or nice, Nash and Eloise are my favorite two people in the world.

But that elf really annoys me.

I couldn't keep the festive doll with the other decorations for fear the kids would discover him, thus ruining the ploy that he appears on the Feast of St. Nicholas. A tradition which includes setting out your shoes—in our case, by the front door—and if you are on Santa's nice list, candy fills your footwear. A kid on the naughty list receives a lump of coal.

My parents used this setup when I was a child, which was long before that shelf elf was even imagined. It was another gimmick propagated by adults to keep their children in line during the holiday season.

"If you're on the naughty list, there's still time to right wrongs."

I've said those very words myself, although my children are not bad kids. They aren't angels by any stretch, but with the year we've had, they're damn near perfect. My ex-husband is the one who belongs on the naughty list. Actually, he belongs on the dirtbag's list, but that's neither here nor there tonight as I tackle my first holiday season without his presence. I want it to be a pleasant Christmas for my little ones. They deserve it.

"Shoes," I mutter aloud, standing in the wintery darkness of ten o'clock in my living room.

Before the kids went to bed, Nash put his gym shoes by the front door beside Eloise's Sherpa-lined boots. She thought St. Nick might bring her more candy if she had taller footwear. *St. Nick is on a budget this year, kiddo.* Of course, she doesn't know the tradition is all make-believe. There isn't a saint named Nick checking in on us. There isn't even a Santa Claus, but I'll wait a few years before breaking her heart on that one.

Lord knows she'll have bigger heartbreaks in her life. I'll shield her as best I can, for as long as I can. But what happens when she's older and on her own? What do I do if she ends up like me, marrying a schmuck?

Mitch hadn't been a schmuck when we married. He was everything I'd been looking for in my early thirties. What does the heart know though, right? Good sex brought us together, but it apparently wasn't good enough because he eventually went elsewhere.

Once. It only happened once.

On a scale of zero times it should have happened, his infidelity occurred one time too many.

His decision shattered me. No marriage is perfect, but that kind of slip-up means there was an issue I hadn't noticed buried underneath the daily life of a married couple with young children. I faulted myself in some ways. Not for him stepping out on me. That was all on him. However, I'd been blinded by a sense of security I had with my ex-husband. And blindsided by his actions.

Now I was forty, wiser, and wary.

And Mitch's construction boots are conspicuously absent from our collection this year.

"Shoes," I mumble again. Snapping my fingers, I recall what I was doing—looking for the elf. Eventually, he'll be placed on top of the fridge or the china cabinet because he needs to be out of reach from Nash, who is only five. At eight years old, Eloise is the one with questions. And shoes are the answer tonight, as the wily elf is in a shoebox on a shelf in my closet—a place the children would never go.

Climbing the stairs of my new-to-us home, I find the little rascal in an old box for heels I no longer own. Once retrieved, I look about the house seeking a good spot to place him. Eloise already wrote him a long list of questions, and I'll need to forage through her letters from last year (also placed in the box) to recall previous answers. She's a smart one, my little girl, and she remembers this shit better than me.

As the litany of her questions spans a sheet of paper front and back, a glass of wine is in order to navigate this process. As a right-handed person, I'll have to disguise my handwriting by using my left hand to write the answers. A full glass of red matches the holiday spirit, I decide, although I don't have a stitch of decoration up in this house yet. I haven't had time. Returning to full-time work after the divorce, plus carpools for extracurricular activities, and the daily grind of getting my children to and from school, then dinner and homework, baths and bedtime routines, I'm beat by the end of the day.

Besides, Thanksgiving was just over a week ago.

After a hardy drink, I focus on the first question.

Number one. Do you like peppermint dick?

I blink, certain I've misread and realize I have.

Do you like peppermint stick?

Sweet baby Jesus in a manger, my imagination got the best of me there, or perhaps it's more my subconscious, as I haven't been with a man in over a year. Feeling dirty and unwanted after what Mitch did, the dry spell hadn't bothered me at first, but now, twelve months later, I miss the sensual touch of another human. My own fingers have worked willingly but not provided the wonder of connecting with someone else.

Number two. How many—

THUNK!

"What the hell?" I glance over my shoulder, peering behind me through the small window in the eating area. Something has just hit my house.

Another thud and then something clatters outside, out of sight of the window.

"When up on the rooftop, there arose such a clatter," I mutter the famous line from Clement Clarke Moore's poem *'Twas the Night Before Christmas."*

Standing, I hold my breath, awaiting another thump when a different thought wafts through my head. The poem is actually titled *A Visit from St. Nick.*

Impossible.

Bemused, I breathily laugh at myself. Clearly, I need more sleep.

Willing my shoulders to relax, I prepare to sit back down when I hear the telltale sign of an aluminum ladder clanking and a light thud of metal connecting with my house again.

On second thought, is the verse *arose such a ladder?*

Shaking my head, I realize I'm losing my mind, but something is definitely banging on the side of my home. With wineglass in hand as if that will protect me, I slip into my own set of Sherpa-lined boots and step out the back door leading to the driveway I share with my neighbor. My single car garage is detached from the house, and I don't park in the slightly leaning building. The space covers bikes, summer furniture, and boxes I haven't unpacked yet. We've only been in the house for seven months.

Standing on the back stoop, I pause. *What am I doing?* I'm a single mother living alone. I shouldn't be out here investigating in the dark.

Then I hear the metal clang of a ladder against the siding once more coming from my front yard and curiosity gets the best of me. Despite the cold, I walk along the side of my home and down the drive toward the front. Cupping the wineglass against my chest, I slowly approach the corner of my house.

"Shit." A deep male voice whispers in the night.

My heartbeat ratchets up a few thumps. *Is someone trying to break in?* They're making quite a racket if that's the case. Not to mention, the only thing of value in this house are my two children *nestled all snug in their beds.*

Rounding the corner, I shout, "What the hell are you doing?"

My sharp voice rips through the quiet night air, causing the man standing on the low roof overhanging my front stoop to slip. With a curse from his lips and the slide of his feet, he scrambles to stay on the narrow strip of roofing. Only his left foot goes over the edge, kicking the gutter. He does an awkward split motion before his body slowly glides to the end of the roof, and his weight takes him off it.

"Oh my God!" I cry out, rushing toward the large body dangling from the overhang. Not more than ten feet from the ground to the start of the incline, his stretched form shows he's roughly six feet plus. He only has a few feet to drop if he lets go of my gutter, which is starting to strain under his weight. He's too far away to reach the ladder, which is propped up on the opposite corner of the overhang. With a swing of long legs in jeans that accentuate the thickness of his thighs and the firmness of his backside, he tucks forward before lunging back and dropping like a cat to the ground, clearing the stairs that descend from the porch. His back remains to me for half a second, and red buffalo check flannel strains over the expanse of thick muscles and flexed biceps in a shirt that hugs his body. Slowly, he turns to face me.

"Nick?" I choke.

With a bright red knit cap on his head, my next-door neighbor stares down at me. He has these intense, dark blue eyes and cheeks like cliffs, matching the mountainous stature of his body. His jaw holds an artful combination of black and white scruff, which is more snow than earth-colored despite his hair still being a shade of charcoal.

And I know these details about Nick, my next-door neighbor, because he's hot with a capital H.

Nick Santos was already living next door when the kids and I moved in. My first interaction with him was when I'd pulled into my driveway one evening to find him making out with a woman against his front door. He didn't break away from her mouth until I'd parked my car, gotten out, and walked toward my front entrance. Only a sliver of grass separates our single car driveways.

I hadn't wanted to look at them, but it was hard to pull away from the sight of his body pressing some woman against the building. His thick leg between her thighs. His hands on her sides. Her arms were around his neck, hands in his hair. He was going for a breast when he pulled back from her and turned his head toward me. Our eyes locked and his gleamed in the early darkness.

Then, like a frightened mouse, I'd scampered toward my house with my head down.

The next time I'd seen him was a week or so later. Shouts and curses came from the house next door. I had been leaving for work sans children, thankfully, as the display in his yard included him standing on the lawn and the woman who I assumed was the one from the week before tossing items out the front door, calling him names I'd never heard and stringing together profanity that might make a sailor blush.

Nick had stood stoic and firm with his legs spread wide, arms crossed, one hand lifted to his chin, slowly stroking thick fingers over that beautiful layering of ink and chrome hair on his jaw.

Hours later, he'd ripped out of his driveway on his motorcycle.

Questions had flitted through my mind at the time. Was she the same woman or someone different? Had he cheated on her or were they the same hot-for-each-other couple from one week ago? The scene had been a reminder of how quickly a relationship can flip. And for some reason I felt sorry for him.

Another week had passed before I'd seen him again, tinkering under the hood of a large pickup truck in his portion of the shared driveway. On that day, I'd been returning from work. Walking up my side of the drive, something prompted me to stop and address him despite us never having exchanged a word previously.

"Are you okay?"

He'd tipped his head. Surprise had been evident in his hard expression before he stood straighter and turned his face in the direction of his front yard.

"Nothing that hasn't happened before," he'd huffed and leaned forward, half-hidden underneath the hood again. "Might have been more effective if it wasn't my house, though."

Puzzled by his explanation, I didn't move from my spot. "Well, I just wanted to make certain you were all right."

He didn't respond at first, but his body stilled once more.

"I'm Holliday," I'd offered. "That's with two l's." There's irony in the name, and I'd waited for him to comment, but he didn't. "My children are Eloise and Nash."

I'd paused, thinking he would introduce himself. Or not.

"Just thought you should know." I'd previously lived in a neighborhood where everyone knew each other's names and the names of their children. It takes a village. Then again, that village knew everyone else's business.

Like how my ex-husband cheated on me while attending a reunion at his alma mater. A rambunctious Big Ten football game led to post-game shenanigans with his college sweetheart.

This new-to-me neighborhood, however, consisted of mainly older homes with elderly residents, and I was out of my element here.

With the growing silence between my neighbor and me, I'd turned on my heels and headed toward my back door.

"I'm Nick," he'd finally stated.

I'd stopped walking but hadn't spun to face him before he added, "You should get your old man to cut the grass."

Glancing at what I could see of my yard, I'd taken offense at several things.

One, I didn't have an old man.

Two, I was aware my grass was overgrown, but I didn't have a mower yet—it was just one more item on a list of growing necessities.

And three, I could take care of my own damn lawn, even if I wasn't certain that was true. I didn't need an old man to do it for me.

"I'll get right on that," I'd muttered, turning only my head over my shoulder and giving him a friendly salute when what I

*really wanted to do was give him the finger. "Nice to meet you."
Sarcasm had dripped in my tone. So much for being neighborly.*

*However, within a few days, the drone of a lawnmower filled
the air, and the sound came particularly close to my home. When
I'd stepped out on my front stoop, Nick was mowing my grass.*

*"What the hell are you doing?" I'd snapped, wondering what
he was playing at by encroaching on my yard. I'd said I'd take
care of it. But I didn't have a viable plan. I'd considered asking
Mitch if I could borrow his lawnmower, the one I'd bought him
two years ago as a Father's Day present, but the thought of asking
Mitch for anything made me sick.*

*The loud hum of the mower cut off, and Nick halted in my
yard. Looking up at me, he clutched the handle of his mower.*

*"I wanted to apologize." Those dark eyes were sparkling
sapphires under the bright summer sunshine. "Your kid told me
you're . . ."*

The unspoken word could be one of many.

Single? Divorced? Helpless?

*"I'll speak to my children about bothering the neighbors." I
crossed my arms and stared back at him.*

*His arms were covered in tattoos, and some even crept up his
neck, sticking out from the collar of his tee, which was plastered
to his chest from the exertion. A giant wet stain formed between
the solid flat of his pecs beneath the cotton. Jeans covered his legs,
accenting the curve of firm thigh muscles. He wore a baseball cap
on his head. He was a beautiful man—slightly dangerous-looking
but gorgeous nonetheless—and he was sweet to cut my grass, even
if it was out of pity.*

"I can pay you," I'd stated.

He'd tipped up a brow. "Consider it my apology."

"For what?" Kissing a woman on his front porch? Fighting with said woman in his yard? Or insulting me about needing a man to tend my lawn?

"I can take care of it." I'd nodded at the grass. I didn't need his apology. I was only being friendly that day when I'd asked about his well-being, foolishly thinking we were kindred spirits through our relationship failures. I had been wrong. He didn't need to prove anything to me.

Heading into the house for my last twenty-dollar bill, I'd returned to find the mower running again. Walking up to him, I held out the money. He'd stilled but didn't cut off the mower this time. He'd stared at the bill in my hand.

"Don't want it!" he'd hollered over the drone of the lawn mower.

"I'd feel better if you take it." My pride was on the line. I'd flicked my wrist once, emphasizing the outstretched twenty.

His gaze lifted, and those sharp eyes met mine. "Buy yourself something pretty with it, and we'll call us even."

Oh, he was smooth. But I wasn't having that nonsense.

I'd folded the bill in my hand and pursed my lips, knowing my next move was bold. I stepped back, allowing him to step forward. Then as he passed me, I slipped the twenty into his back pocket, getting an unintentional swipe of the firmness of one globe, stretching worn denim over his ass.

He'd stopped abruptly, twisting his upper body and staring down at my retreating hand.

"Buy yourself something pretty," I'd taunted and stomped away from him. I wasn't going to owe him, neighbor or not.

That was back in June.

In the cold of December, the night air is seeping through my thin, long-sleeved shirt and pajama shorts. What was I thinking stepping out here wearing boots and wielding a wineglass?

"Where's your jacket?" Nick snipes, stepping toward me, hands reaching forward to rub up and down my arms. I'd pulled them in close, huddling them against my chest as I hopped from foot to foot, waiting for him to explain what he'd been doing on my roof.

However, the freezing chill skittering over my skin disappears under the warmth of his calloused palms. His proximity infuses my entire body with a rush of heat, that ignites something in the depths of my cold bones. The faint scent of bayberry and snow tickles my nose, awakening all my senses. Forget my wine, I'm intoxicated by his nearness.

"I heard a noise," I stammer, struggling to remember what he asked me.

"Sorry about that." He removes his hands, and instantly, I miss the heat of his touch.

He tips his head, sheepishly peering down at the ground.

"What are you doing out here?" I nod at my roof, noting the ladder and some tools plus a cardboard box, resting on the shingles.

"I was hanging Christmas lights."

"On *my* house?"

"You're bringing down the block," he teases as he'd done the remainder of the summer when I still hadn't purchased a lawnmower.

My dad eventually bought me a mower from a garage sale in September, but as I struggled to start the thing, Nick appeared and told me he'd upkeep the lawn as he had most of the previous months. He continued to refuse my money.

"I hadn't gotten to it." The phrase was becoming the story of my life.

For the sake of my children, my intentions for the holiday season were well-meaning, but I haven't decorated yet. I haven't purchased any gifts. I haven't planned any seasonal activities. As a single mom, working full-time, I was doing the best I could living on a budget of time and finances. Which roughly translated to, I didn't have the *ho-ho-ho* energy I've had in years' past.

My Christmas spirit was waning this year, like that one pesky bulb causing an entire strand of lights to go out.

However, as Nick looks at me, his eyes twinkle like the little blue lights I've seen in other people's yards. And a teeny-tiny spark inside me wants to do better. Be better.

"What are *you* doing out here? It's freezing." His hands return to my arms, rubbing up and down once again. Immediately, the warmth melts over my skin, heating me up like a cozy winter fire.

"I thought you were the sugar plum fairy breaking in."

Nick laughs, hearty and full, rich like the wine in my glass.

"You don't need to do this," I remind him, repeating what I'd said dozens of times to him over the past few months. He feels sorry for me. That's why he does what he does. I'm that single mother neighbor who will one day let cats overrun her home when her children grow older and leave her alone, forgetting she exists.

The thought is pathetic and sobering.

"I want to," he states, as he's said often enough.

"Nash and Eloise will love it," I say, hoping my children's happiness means something to him. He's friendly with them. He even played catch with Nash a few times this fall when Mitch didn't show up for his scheduled weeknight visits. Nick also praised Eloise's chalk drawings, allowing her to overtake his driveway when ours is full of sketches.

"I want *you* to love it," he says, his eyes still on me.

I'd offer to pay him for the lights or his time, but I already know he'll reject the gesture. After my bold move last summer to slip a twenty in his pocket, I've never attempted to touch him again. I've made him cookies and casseroles, bought pots with flowers for his porch, and left him a case of beer on occasion. I didn't know how else to repay him for his kindness.

"It will look beautiful." I'm not really certain how it will look, but the roofline was made for Christmas lights. If he edges the front porch overhang and wraps lights over the dormers on the taller roof like he did his own home, the twinkling magic will bring cheer to my little house.

I like the place with its three small bedrooms on the second floor and its subtle front stoop raised up a few steps as typical Chicago homes are. Our previous home in the suburbs was double the size with manicured landscaping and a koi pond. Still, this place is mine and I smile in spite of myself.

"Thank you." My voice is quiet as my teeth chatter.

"Get inside." He winks with a tilt of his head toward the front door. "I'll try not to make too much noise."

"Try not to fall off the roof," I warn with a laugh in my throat.

"You startled me." His eyes narrow a bit, focusing on my face until his gaze drifts to the pebbled nipples poking out beneath my thin sleep shirt. He doesn't take his gaze from my chest.

I breathily answer him. "You surprised me."

His Adam's apple bobs, and he pulls his head upward, turning to give me the side of his face. "Go inside, Holliday." His deep voice roughens, and his jaw clenches.

The strangest sensation washes over me. I want to kiss up the column of his throat, outline the edge of his jaw with my lips, and climb his body like the evergreen he is.

The thought isn't entirely offhand as I've had several similar fantasies throughout the summer and into fall about him. I'm highly attracted to my neighbor, though it's ridiculous to feel this way.

"You're going to catch a cold," he adds, breaking into my vision of slipping my arms inside his red-checked flannel and pressing my cool tits to his warm chest.

His words are a reminder he isn't attracted to me.

He just feels sorry for the single mom next door.

Chapter 2

As if I'm not already a glutton for punishment, I'd volunteered to work the local church's breakfast with Santa.

Mitch assured me he would attend to sit with the kids so I could scramble around the community center, making certain every table has a coffee carafe and a plate of donut holes. I'm told a fireman dresses up as Santa and allows the children to sit on his lap and tell him what they want for Christmas.

"You should see this guy," one of the other moms warns me. "I want to sit on his lap."

I have no idea why she'd say such a thing until Santa appears, looking a little too sexy and a whole lot of naughty.

He isn't bothering with a pillow inside his red jacket but allows his biceps to bulge in the tight costume. His waistline cinched by a thick black belt, lies flat suggesting his abs are firm. The soft fabric pants hug his thighs, accentuating a fit backside, and his boots are made for a motorcycle more than a sleigh. The white scruff on his face is full enough but not solid white Santa quality. Hints of black rest on a jaw that is more cliff-edge than rounded and rosy. A pair of wire-rimmed eyeglasses does nothing to soften his appearance. The stocking cap on his head helps only the slightest.

"Hot damn, I was hoping it would be him again," another mother adds, rushing past me to pass out plates of eggs and sausage.

I watch our Santa take a seat in a chair on a low stage. Children line up with excitement while the mothers all tip their heads, and husbands cough to regain their wives' attention. As I cross the room, I feel eyes on me. Glancing up, I notice hot Santa tracking my movements while a child sits on one of his firm thighs.

Yeah, I might want to sit on Santa's lap as well.

Only what would I ask for this year?

My eyes leap to Mitch, sitting with our children, who are both staring at the man in red. Mitch is focused on something underneath the table. The closer I near, the more I assume he's texting someone.

Dammit. Why can't the man engage with his children?

Taking another second, I glance up at the fake father of Christmas. His eyes widen, and then he winks.

I halt.

I know that wink.

That twitch of lids with lashes a woman would kill for. Crystal blue eyes that haunt my dreams and play out in my fantasies.

Nick?

"Holli." My name from Mitch's mouth brings my attention to the table where my children continue to eagerly look at the stage, and Mitch sets his phone face down on the table.

"Hey, guys." My voice is a little too loud. "Having fun?"

I don't address my ex because I don't care if he's enjoying himself. These are his children, and it's Christmastime.

"We could use some more coffee," Mitch states.

And I'd love to pour the hot liquid right over his head. Who is *we*? Our children don't drink such a thing. Ignoring him, I address Eloise. "Have you been up to see Santa yet?"

"Daddy says we need to wait. The line is too long."

While the line is long, people need to get in it to see the man. There's no special treatment here.

"It will go down in a little bit," Mitch says to our daughter. "We'll get up when there are fewer people."

I sigh.

"What?" he snaps at me.

His privilege is showing, but I'm not eager to argue with him, especially not in front of the church community. My parents belong here, and everyone knows my story. When Mitch and I split, my mom and dad wanted me to move in with them, but I just couldn't. I couldn't go home at forty years old with two children and an unused college degree that my father had said was a waste of money in the first place.

"What can you do with an English major?"

I'd quickly learned—not much. Instead, I'd worked in a bank as a teller for years before meeting Mitch. He'd convinced me to stay at home once we had children. After being out of the workforce for nearly a decade, my return to a bank hadn't been a smooth transition. I hated my job.

Mitch is still staring at me, but I ignore him and address Nash. "What are you going to ask Santa for, buddy?"

"A Zlot 720."

Mitch and I have put off the purchase of the gaming system. I argued Nash was still too young for video games. Mitch disagreed. Eventually, he bulldozed my opinion and promised Nash that *Santa will bring it.*

Only, who was Santa this year? Mitch never did the Christmas shopping. I did. I also wrapped all the presents, set them underneath the tree, took holiday pictures, sent out Christmas cards, and made both the morning breakfast and a holiday feast.

I blow out a breath at the reminder of all the things I used to do.

This year, Mitch and I agreed that Santa would bring presents to *my* new house, and Mitch could come over in the morning to witness the kids seeing their gifts. He's made no attempt to find the gaming system, though, and he hasn't offered to share the expense of the nearly four-hundred-dollar item.

"Be extra good, and Santa will bring it, pal," Mitch states again to our five-year-old, ruffling his hair.

Nash beams at Mitch like he's a hero, and I curse the devil who is my ex because he's making promises that can't be kept. I'm having trouble finding the gaming system. The highly sought-after present is back-ordered online, and every store sells out as soon as they get a shipment in.

"Mitch," I grumble.

"What?" he says, like he's innocent.

What? It was only once. Why are you overreacting? It was a mistake.

Only, that mistake was now living with him in my old house.

"Nothing," I grit out, turning away from him, ignoring Santa Nick as well, and crossing the crowded community room for the kitchen. Slamming the swivel doors open a little too aggressively, I stop short once I enter and two other mothers look up at me.

"Exes," I huff. One nods to agree. The other gives me a sympathetic smile.

"Ask Santa for a new man," the first says.

"I don't need a new man," I whisper as I close my eyes and fist my fingers.

"That's too bad," a deep voice brushes the hairs on the back of my neck. My lids pop open, but I don't turn to face him. Instead, my gaze lands on the two women on the other side of the kitchen.

"I needed a break," he offers to the women over my shoulder. "Would you mind giving us a minute?"

I have no doubt the *us* means I'm to stay, and I couldn't attempt to leave anyway as my feet feel pinned to the floor.

Once both women scuttle around us, Nick's hands come to my shoulders, keeping my back to him. "What happened out there?"

"Nothing," I mumble, lowering my head.

"Holliday." My name from his lips is like a sip of wine. So full. So rich. So tangy on the tongue.

"My ex is an asshole." I shrug with Nick's hands still on me. My response is the long and short of it. Ten years of marriage all down the drain with a keg of beer and a football game.

Nick remains quiet behind me. I should really turn to face him. I don't know why I'm hiding in this kitchen or why he followed me in here.

"If you don't want a new man for Christmas, what do you want?"

I snort, and off the cuff state a worry on my mind. "I'd like for the old one to pay my mortgage."

On that note, I spin to face Nick, and his eyes meet mine, searching them. I'm certain he reads everything. Pathetic. Desperate. Incapable. Unable to take care of things despite always preaching I can.

My parents are pushing harder for me to move in with them. They know I'm financially strained, taking on a new house with a single income paying barely over minimum wage. Mitch's child support has been spotty at best, and I don't have the means to take him to court again. I don't want us to come to extreme measures. Not yet.

I shrug again while Nick watches me. His stare is eerie and strange, and eventually, my brows pinch.

"That was too much information. Just ignore me. I'm in a . . ."—*a funk? A phase?* I thought I'd be so much more at forty—"a mood. Bah humbug."

Nick lightly chuckles. "I don't think that's it."

He's right. That isn't it. I'm lonely, and I'm sad. The holidays are wearing on me when I don't want them to. This is the happiest time of the year, right? I have children who make this time magical, but I'm finding it difficult to muster the jolly brightness I need.

I'd like a little seasonal cheer for me, and it's not in the form of something bought in a store.

"You need a night off," Nick states.

I laugh, waving a hand to dismiss the thought. "A night off? What's that?" I pause. *Maybe next year?* "I'll be fine." It's true. I will be.

Nick doesn't believe my answer, and why would he? He mows my grass. He moves my garbage cans. When he'd hung Christmas lights on my gutters, my children were convinced the fucking elf did it for them.

And Nick . . . he just played along when Nash told him the next day the pimp of an imp delivered the magic to our roof.

"If you ask Santa nicely, he might give you anything you wish for," Nick teases while his eyes don't leave my face.

An anxious giggle ripples up my throat. I couldn't possibly tell this uncharacteristically sexy Santa what I really want for Christmas.

"Just ask." The drop in his voice is like a live wire right down the middle of my body and straight between my thighs. My core drums *ba-rumba-dum-dum,* and my mouth goes dry. I'd like to be naughty, so very naughty with him.

My breath hitches with the thought, and Nick's eyes widen at the intake of air.

"Tell me, Holliday, have you been *naughty* or nice this year?" There's no chance of answering him truthfully, and I'm saved from response when he leans toward me and winks again before spinning on his heels and exiting the kitchen.

My heart hammers, and I lift a hand to my chest, feeling the *thumpity-thump.*

Dear Santa, can I have Nick naked underneath my Christmas tree, please?

A sharp, sarcastic laugh bursts from me in strange relief at the fantasy and the fact I'm kind of not joking.

+ + +

When Mitch flakes on taking the kids for the remainder of the day as he promised, I ask my parents to watch them. My mom offers to have them spend the night. The nearly twenty-four-hour reprieve sounds like a godsend. While I'd love nothing more than to spend the remainder of the day taking a bath, a nap, and binge-watching television, I decide to brave the stores instead for the damn gaming system Mitch promised Nash. Eloise will be easier to please as she wants a special look-alike doll that I can order online and have shipped to the bank, so she won't see the package.

As I battle the mall, searching all the locations that boast having the Zlot 720s, I eventually end up at a technology superstore. Turning down an aisle, as directed by one of the less-than-enthusiastic holiday helpers, I nearly collide with a large body.

"I'm so sorry," I state, holding up my hands to prevent a full collision.

"Holliday?" The deep masculine voice causes me to look up into twinkling blue eyes.

"Nick."

"What are you doing?"

Glancing around the aisle, I answer with the obvious. "Christmas shopping." Then I think again. "Actually, I'm driving myself mad because my ex promised my son a Zlot 720, which is now up to me to purchase and impossible to find."

Peering over Nick's shoulder, I see two women fighting over the last gaming system on a flatbed cart. The poor salesperson hardly had time to finish pushing it down the aisle.

"I hate the holidays," I mutter.

"You don't mean that," Nick says, tilting his head. "It's the most wonderful time of the year." His encouragement hints a little at sarcasm.

"How is this bringing me cheer?" I wave at the shelves around me, then shake my head. "You know what? Forget I said that. I'm sorry. If you enjoy this kind of thing, then ho-ho-ho." My voice drops, and Nick laughs hefty like his belly jiggles, although I doubt his firm abs even wiggle.

"A Zlot 720, you say?" He arches a brow. "I might know a guy." The statement sounds ominous and rather gangster, but the wide grin exposing his white teeth flips my mood.

If his statement was true, I might kiss him. Mistletoe not required.

A moment of comforting silence passes between us with his dark blue eyes on me. Finally, he says, "How about a hot chocolate?"

"That's . . . festive, but you don't need to—"

"I want to." His raised hand emphasizes his honesty, and then he slides that same hand down my arm and tangles his fingers with mine. "Please."

Before I fully accept his invitation, he tugs me forward, leading me out of the store and down the outdoor walkway to a donut shop across the parking lot. And all the while, I can only concentrate on how easily he took my hand, entwining our fingers like we're a couple. The heat of his palm infuses mine, causing my heart to nearly beat out of my chest while he's the epitome of calmness.

Nothing happening here. Just holding hands with my hot neighbor.

"I love their hot chocolate," I say, finally finding my voice as we enter the place.

"I know."

This brings me up short. "How?"

Nick and I don't speak often. He works in my yard. I leave him surprises on his stoop. But we don't hang out. We don't exchange phone numbers or share long conversations. I know he's a fireman because I've seen him in his uniform. He owns a motorcycle, a large pickup truck, and a house. That's the extent of my knowledge. A woman in his life? I haven't seen another one at his home since last summer, but that doesn't mean after dark someone isn't over there with him, pinned against an inside wall, allowing him to kiss her silly.

"Eloise told me. I asked her how you like your coffee once, and she told me you don't drink it. Only hot chocolate on occasion. Today seems like an occasion." He chuckles.

"If you want to offer me something stronger, I'd take it," I quip, before I can rein the comment in.

He arches a brow as we near the counter. "Really?"

I shrug. What am I suggesting? He buy me a drink? Ask me out on a date? Bring *me* to his house and kiss me senseless? I'm being ridiculous again.

Nick orders hot drinks—chocolate for me, coffee for him—and we take a seat at a small table in the corner.

"So, what can I do to turn your bah humbug spirit around?" he teases me with a smile.

Buying myself time, I lift my steamy mug and sip. Whip cream tips my nose and I swipe at the sweetness before popping my finger in my mouth. Nick watches the move, eyes darkening like coal.

"You've already done enough. The lights on the house really are beautiful. Thanks again for playing along with Nash and letting him think our elf did it."

"Ah, the elf. He's always watching, isn't he?" Nick winks.

God, that wink. "Thank goodness ours stays on the first floor," I state.

"Meaning?" Nick tilts his head, lifting his own mug of coffee.

"Don't need him seeing what I do in my bedroom."

Sprays of coffee shoot from Nick's mouth.

Why the hell would I say that? "Forget I said that," I blurt, handing over my napkin as Nick swipes at his lips. Quickly, I attempt to change the subject. "Tell me how you ended up playing Santa this morning."

He straightens in his seat a second, forehead furrowing until recognition comes. "Oh, you mean the volunteering . . . well, I'm a fireman. We take different locations around the city and dress up like the big man. I've gotten the church two years in a row."

"Why don't I remember you from last year?"

"Maybe you weren't paying attention?" His brows salaciously wiggle as he looks at me over the rim of his mug before attempting another sip.

At the Santa breakfast last year, Mitch and I weren't separated yet. The news of his infidelity came about during a New Year's Eve party. His friends joked about *that* weekend. Someone asked him about Paige.

32

"You okay?" Nick interjects.

"Yeah, just . . ." I don't really want to talk about my ex. I definitely don't want to bash him to another man, but I'm angry with Mitch, especially with his newest failure being a promised Christmas gift. I shouldn't be surprised. He reneged on our wedding vows. Somehow making a false promise to our son feels just as bad. "It's different this year, for the kids. And Mitch is just being Mitch."

"Mitch is your ex, right?"

I nod. "I suppose you know a little bit about awful exes." I recall the woman tossing stuff out his front door.

"Me?" He scoffs. "I've never been married. Not even in a long-term relationship."

"But the woman last summer— Never mind. It's none of my business."

He tilts his head. "The woman last summer? She wasn't anyone special. She was a snowball in hell. No chance of getting what she wanted."

Before I truly consider the question, I ask, "What did she want?"

A sly smile curls the corner of his mouth, and my gaze drifts between the smirk and that heavier beard on his face. My fingers itch to comb through the hairs. Is it coarse? Is it soft? How would it feel between my legs? That last question has me squirming in my seat.

"She wanted my interest. And she didn't like that it was turned toward my new next-door neighbor."

What? He can't be serious. He isn't interested in me. "I didn't mean to ruin anything for you." Although, I have no idea why I'm apologizing.

His smexy grin grows. His eyes mischievously spark like he has a secret. "Nothing ruined."

"Too bad for her." That woman has no idea how crazy her envy had been. I'm nothing to my neighbor. I'm just the woman living next door.

Nick hums.

"So, a fireman?" I question to redirect our conversation again. "How'd that come about?"

"I grew up someplace constantly cold, and I have a mad respect for fire. When I moved to Chicago in my twenties, I decided to become a fireman. Been loving my job ever since." Nick is easily around forty, so he's been dedicated to his line of work for a long time.

"What do you respect about fire?"

"The heat." His eyes flicker, a flame glinting within them as he stares at me.

"My house doesn't have a fireplace."

"Mine does. You can come over anytime and let mine warm you up. Maybe share a stronger drink with me." He lifts his mug to salute me.

Glancing down at my hot chocolate, I note most of the whip cream has melted, making it easier to drink without fear of white fluff ending up on my nose. Lifting the mug, I take another sip, savoring the rich chocolate flavor over my tongue. Drinking it reminds me of Nick's voice—warm, soothing, seductive even.

When I lower the mug, he chuckles.

"What?"

He swipes at my nose this time and brings his finger back to his mouth, taking his time to suck at the tip before popping it free. "You had whip cream on your nose again."

34

"If you hadn't already noticed, I can be kind of a hot mess at times."

"No mess." He watches me. "Just hot."

I laugh. He's so smooth with the lines but he's also full of *coal*. Nick has naughty-ish written all over him, and admittedly, I'd like him to write a little bit of it on me.

Could I visit his house? Would his fireplace warm me? Would he? If he wants to share a drink with me, would I really be his flavor?

On that thought, I guzzle the remainder of my drink, drowning out my horny thoughts.

"So, what's on your shopping list?"

"Oh." I shift my purse and rummage through the chaos inside, pulling out a few receipts and several lists, laying the thin strip of paper on the table.

"You know, most people make lists in their phone," he teases.

"Yeah, well, I still like paper and pens."

"Colored ones, I see." Nick tips a brow and I look down to see a short list written in red and green marker.

"I—" I stare at the To-Do list I'd made the night I was answering Eloise's note to our elf. I'd already forgotten about it as I put it in my purse with the gift list. However, the To-Do list has a word crossed off and simply states: A Holiday DO list.

Nick's fingers press against the list, and he slides it toward him. "What's this?"

He scans the list before reading aloud the points. "Buy presents." He lifts his head. "But you've crossed off buy and wrote in be."

I shrug. "I guess I was hoping for a new tradition. Christmas is really for children and shopping is kind of a drag. With our new circumstances, I wanted to do more things. Be more present not just give my kids toys."

Nick watches me. "Christmas isn't about age. It's to remind us to be young at heart."

"Well, I'm missing the youthful joy this year." I don't mean to sound like such a downer but I'm just not feeling the *fa-la-la-la*.

Nick stares down at the list again, forehead furrowing. "You took your kids to the breakfast."

"That's just it. I was *at* the breakfast, but I wasn't present with them. Mitch got to sit at the table with the kids while I worked." And my kids didn't look very excited with their father in charge.

Nick looks up at me and nods. "Okay. So, what else is on the list?" He glances down and reads out loud the remaining items and my modifications.

"Wrap gifts. Wrap someone in a hug."

"Send gifts. Send Peace."

"Shop for food. Donate food."

"Make cookies. Make love." He pauses and glances up at me again, a brow arching once more.

My face heats. It's certainly been a while regarding that last point.

The list isn't exactly comprehensive nor is it a mission statement. It's simply a list where I marked off the things written in green to modify them in red.

"See the lights." Nick reads the final item and looks at me again, those eyes intense once more. "Be the light."

Unease colors my cheeks, and I slide the list toward me before folding it in half. "I'd seen something like this list on Instagram or Pinterest or somewhere creative like that. I guess I was just playing around with the words after I made my initial list." I don't know why I'm defending myself.

"It's a great Do list." Sincerity fills his voice, but I'm still unsettled that he read it, as if it's a secret journal entry and I don't even journal.

+ + +

Nick and I part ways when he tells me he has somewhere to be. I fumble through, "Of course," and "Thank you," before hanging my head and heading home.

After my shopping trip proves unproductive, I take the bath I wanted and soak for an hour, but my body feels more alive than relaxed. Just beneath my skin is this yearning sensation. A need for something . . . or rather someone.

I shouldn't do it. It shouldn't be a thing, but my fingers coast between my breasts and down my midsection. Fumbling through coarse hair, I curl over the mound and close my eyes when my fingertips find that sensitive nub. With two fingertips and a little bit of pressure, the fantasy begins.

Nick on his knees.

Nick between my thighs.

Nick—

The doorbell rings. And like I've been caught with my fingers in a Christmas cookie tin, I pull them back and sit upright in the tub, sloshing water around me.

Holding my breath, I wait for whomever it is, that I obviously cannot see, to leave my front stoop. I'm not expecting anyone, and I typically don't open the door to strangers, especially when it's only a solicitor or political promoter.

However, the doorbell rings again and then a heavy rap sounds loudly through the house. As I've been in the tub long enough and my little naughty Nick fantasy was a bust, I climb out and quickly dry off. I don't have a robe, so I grab the oversized flannel shirt hanging on the back of the door and shove my arms into it, using it like a wintery wrap.

When another rap rattles the door, I rush down the stairs and peek through the transom window at the top, immediately recognizing the red cap. With a fierce tug, I open the barrier and clutch my flannel shirt.

"Nick?" I'm breathless from racing. "Is everything okay?"

His gaze roams over me. Taking in my hair which is tucked up in a messy bun on my head and my shirt which isn't buttoned but wrapped around me by my arms crossing over my midsection to keep it closed. My legs are bare. I'm also not wearing any underwear and I'm praying all my bits are covered.

"Was I interrupting something?"

Yes! My little daydream about him but perhaps he read my thoughts through our homes and across the drive and came over to demand I knock it off.

"No." I'm still out of breath from rushing to answer the door. "I was just getting out of the tub." I swipe a hand up the back of my hair, tucking in loose strands while clutching at the side of my flannel with my other hand.

"Sorry I missed it." Nick's eyes twinkle.

The innuendo in his tone isn't missed, and my legs tremble, desperate to come together to quell the ache that still lingers from the interruption.

"Do you always answer the door dressed like this?" His eyes scan up my body once more causing my skin to pebble.

"I don't own a robe."

38

Nick's face slowly morphs from flirtatious to something more somber. His eyes narrow. "Are you alone?" The question is more of a suggestion, almost as if he's hoping I was alone in that tub versus sharing the space with someone.

"Of course." The answer is too quick, like I'm guilty when all I'd been doing was giving my thoughts over to fantasies of him. "What did you need?"

In all the months I've lived here, Nick has never knocked on my door to borrow some sugar or ask for bread. Not that I'd do such a thing to him, but there were times in my old house when I'd be out of stock on sugar the night before Eloise needed cookies for school and Mitch wasn't home to run to the store. Or there was that time when I didn't know I didn't have a spare loaf of bread in the freezer and asked my generous neighbor if she could make two extra sandwiches for my kids for summer camp.

"My plans for this evening were cancelled."

"Oh, too bad." Poor woman, whoever she was.

"I suddenly have two tickets for something, and I thought you might like to go. You mentioned earlier how Nash and Eloise are with your parents for the night."

"Oh, well, thanks but I'm not really dressed, and I don't have anyone to ask—"

Nick's deep chuckle abruptly cuts me off. "Get dressed. And go out with me."

I stare at him, as if he's Santa asking me to lead his sleigh. Did my next-door neighbor just ask me out on a date? Is this some kind of Christmas prank?

It hits me that I'm a substitute for whoever he intended to take somewhere and while my excitement rose at the prospect of Nick asking me out, the crash that follows at the thought of being secondary is like the man in the red sleigh colliding into my roof instead of softly landing on it.

"I don't—"

Nick raises his glove-covered hand to stop my refusal. "Just get dressed." He steps forward, forcing me back into my house where the cold from outside finally hits me, especially between my thighs and along my bare legs.

"As much as I really like what you're wearing"—he draws a hand up and down before me as he closes the door behind him—"We'll be outside, so you should probably bundle up."

The idea that I'm standing in for someone else doesn't settle well with me, but the prospect of a night out has me curious.

"Where are we going?" I tilt my head, taking in the heavy coat he wears with a scarf around his neck and the bright red cap on his head.

"Let me surprise you."

He has no idea I'm already surprised. Shocked that he's asking me out. Stumped that he's standing in my house. I don't think he's ever been in here.

"Maybe some long underwear, if you have it. Definitely layers with thick socks and boots." His eyes scan my exposed legs again. The edge of my flannel shirt only hits my upper thighs.

"Okay. Give me a second." I scrape hair up the back of my neck again, futilely tucking pieces into the messy bun.

"I'll wait." His salacious tone must be my imagination but the ripple up my middle is like drinking something cold too quickly. The rush is a buzz. And on shaky legs, I thunder up my stairs to get dressed.

Chapter 3

Being as I didn't know where we were going or what we were doing, I dressed in layers as Nick suggested but layering isn't exactly sexy. My leggings felt bulky with long underwear underneath them, plus I wear thick boot socks that peek out the top of my leather riders. My bulky, long coat and a thick scarf plus a knit hat to cover my hair because it was a riot of waves after being tucked in a bun, completed my outfit.

Nick opened the door of his truck for me and even helped me up. Once I'm shut inside, he rounds the hood and enters, starting the engine and cranking up the heat. A woman screeches through the sound system about being woken up inside.

"Evanescence fan?" I arch a brow at him.

He chuckles. "Are you?"

"Not exactly."

"I bet you like all those Christmas carols. Been listening since Halloween on that station that pushes the season to October." He guffaws again.

"Yeah, not exactly." I stare out the window knowing he's only teasing and means well but I've struggled to listen to holiday music this year.

"Hey," Nick softly says, drawing my attention back to him. "I'm only joking."

"I know. It's just . . ." I wasn't certain I could explain myself but figured what the hell. "Some songs are so sad. Take "I'll Be Home for Christmas." I mean, I just want to cry every time I hear it. Or "White Christmas." You just know that's for military guys who can't spend the holidays at home."

Nick stares out the windshield as I wind up.

"And then there's the questionable ones like "Baby, It's Cold Outside" which is still a favorite, but you can't say that anymore. Maybe he just really wants her to stay. And she really doesn't want to go.""

The corner of Nick's mouth curls.

"Or that flipping "All I Want For Christmas Is You" song. Could it get any cheesier? How did it become the quintessential Christmas tune?"

"You got something against Mariah Carey?" Nick laughs.

"Do you have something for her?"

He laughs harder. "Can't say she's exactly my type."

I scoff. The woman he had plastered to his door last summer could have been the famous singer's twin. All long legs and big boobs and curves like a toboggan run. If she wasn't his type, I'm definitely not his thing. Not that I need to be his thing, I just . . . *oh, never mind.*

"Anyway, I just don't seem to be in the mood for Christmas songs this year."

"Because of your ex?" Nick's voice is serious while he switches on his blinker, and we curl onto the highway heading north.

"No." *Maybe?* "I don't know." I sigh. "It isn't Mitch specifically. In fact, I don't want to give him credit for anything lately. It's just all this . . . holiday stuff. I used to love Christmas. It's the happiest time of the year." I mock. "But something has taken the jingle out of my bells."

Nick laughs again, harder still.

I squint at the darkness around us and the lights of passing cars. "Maybe I've just turned into a giant icicle." *I'm frozen inside.*

"Then we need to warm you back up to the ideals of this time."

"Idea, you mean," I state, as if I'm correcting one of my children when they mispronounce a word.

"No, the ideals. The beliefs. The beauty of Christmas."

Glancing over at him, I tilt my head. "You don't seem like the I-believe-in Santa-Claus type, even if you play one in real life." I laugh at my own joke.

"I do believe in Santa Claus." His voice is level.

I choke on my laughter when I realize he isn't kidding. "You can't be serious?"

"Why not? What's wrong with a little magic in our lives? A little hope?"

This from an alternative rock lover? The stereotype isn't fair. Who am I, with my shitty anti-Christmas mood, to judge him? If a grown man, who looks like a biker, yet dresses as Santa, wants to believe in the mystical man, so be it.

The subtle scream of a heavy metal song on low volume fills the cab as we continue down the road until Nick hits his blinker again, signaling his exit from the highway. To my right is a long brick wall with bright lights illuminating the name Chicago Botanic Garden which isn't officially located in Chicago city proper but is still linked with our fabulous city.

"I've always wanted to go to their Winter Wonderland Light Show," I admit, as we pull up the exit ramp.

Nick hums as we turn in the direction of the garden and then gets into the line of cars waiting to enter the area.

"Nick," I shriek with sudden excitement. "You had a date for the Winter Wonderland Light Show?" I sigh as we near the parking lot attendant. "Poor woman who missed this," I add.

Nick aligns with the attendant, pays the parking fee, and pulls forward into the lot. He purses his lips, twisting them side to side before saying, "My *date* was my mom. She has the flu."

"Your mom?" I cough on the excuse. He's using his mom as a cover for his canceled date.

Nick parks in a spot but doesn't cut the engine. Instead, he hits the phone button on the dashboard and a dial tone fills the truck cab. The contact on the dash reads Mom.

Oh God.

"Nick?" A groggy sounding female answers on the third ring.

"Hey, Mom, how you feeling?" Nick immediately asks.

"Honey, I'm not doing any better than two hours ago when you called me. I'm sorry I had to cancel, but I just don't think I should be out in the cold."

"I don't want you in the cold either."

The concern in his voice melts my icicle heart a little. He cares about his mom and that's a huge check in the good guy column.

"I'm sorry you paid for the tickets and now you've lost out on using them."

"Actually, Mom, I found someone else to take with me." Nick faces me, dangles his wrist over the steering wheel and arches his brow. "I asked my neighbor."

"You're on a date?" The excitement in his mom's voice crackles under the smokiness of what I imagine is a sore throat. "Oh my gosh. Is this the single mom you said was hot—"

"Okay, Mom. You're on speaker phone, and I gotta go."

No, don't go. I want to hear what his mom was about to say. Am I the single mom she mentioned? Was she about to say he calls me a hot *mess*? Or was it something else? Does Nick think I'm good looking? He called me hot before, but he was joking, right?

And what's with all the questions? I'm not a teenager desperate to know does he like me, check yes or no, in the appropriate box of my classroom note.

"Why am I on speaker phone?" His mom interjects. "And why are you even calling me if you're on a date? You really are out of practice and—"

"I'll call you later, Ma. Love you."

"Don't call me later." She chuckles but it sounds like a barking dog. "And love you, too."

Nick presses END on the call and pushes the ignition button to turn off the truck.

"Did you really just call your mom?"

Nick focuses on me. "Didn't want you to think you were a replacement date."

"I am a replacement, though," I tease.

He smiles sweetly. "No one replaces my mom. But I'm happy you were available to come with me."

"Well, I am a single *mom*." I emphasize, recalling what his mother said. "And did your mom call me hot?" My face heats as I repeat her words.

"Actually, *I* said you were hot. And I've told you that on more than one occasion." Nick opens his door on those words, and I'm left a little stunned. *He thinks I'm good looking?*

It's not that I think I'm bad looking, I'm just kind of a mess lately. I don't always eat well and sometimes I have a stain on my shirt I didn't realize was there until I'm already at work. Other times, I only have mascara on one eye because I've been interrupted while putting on my makeup in the morning by one of the kids. I might even have a hole in one sock and had to wear it anyway because I haven't gotten to the laundry.

While Nick comes round the truck, I slide to my door and open it. Nick steps forward and places his hands on my hips, lifting me down from the cab like I weight nothing, even under all these layers. When my feet hit the ground, he remains close, and I get a whiff of a bayberry and snow scent coming off him. With our bodies close, our warm exhalations intermingle in the cold night air. The merging of our breaths is like the whisper of a kiss.

Nick abruptly lets me go, takes a step back, and simply asks in a gruff voice, "Ready to see the lights?"

"I'm so ready." And while I've said it breathlessly, my heart races and my face heats again at the possibility this is a date. Even as a substitute for his mom, I'm on my first date in years.

The entrance to the garden is crowded and Nick takes my mitten-covered hand in his leather-gloved one to draw me around a group taking their time to enter.

As we approach the first water garden, I imagine the wistful intimacy of being the only two people present. We'd be able to stop and admire the dancing lights over the pond without a large, rambunctious crowd dampening the romantic effect.

Still, we slow to take in each display of hopping lights and swirling streams of illumination synchronized to holiday music. The movements remind me of Disneyworld with its thematic tunes orchestrated to fireworks or coordinated with images projected on a wall of water.

Eventually, we break free of the crowd for a moment and wander down a path that looks like thousands of fireflies flitting among the evergreens. I stop abruptly and stare.

"How did they do that?" I whisper in wonder as the lights speckle the trees like miniature fairy-winged bugs that couldn't possibly be present in such cold temperatures.

An instrumental of "Christmas Time Is Here" comes on.

"I love this song," I quietly add, negating my earlier argument against holiday music.

Nick arches a brow at me, adding a smirk at the classic from "A Charlie Brown Christmas." "You love this?"

Chewing at my lower lip, I nod, suppressing a giggle. Standing here in the dark, watching pinpricks of light float around us, I feel lighter, almost giddy, and with the piano-heavy song playing I itch to dance.

Raising my arms, I sway my hips and hum along.

Nick looks around as if he's searching for someone, then his hand comes to my hip and he's gently pushing me forward before he steps over the low chain barrier that edges the path to keep people out of the gardens.

"What are you doing?" I hush-whisper, glancing over my shoulders as Nick fists the edge of my coat in his fingers and tugs me forward until we're slipping between the evergreen trees. He gently pulls until we're in the middle of the setting, where we definitely should not be.

"Nick?" I scold.

"Shush." He pauses and tips back his head. "Look around."

Brushing off the fact this burly looking man just shushed me, I tilt back my head and look up as dots of light dance around us. It's like standing in the middle of a dark forest in summertime when the fireflies come out. Or in the middle of a snow globe filled with dancing light.

"Be the light," Nick murmurs.

Be the light. The phrase from my list.

Lowering my head, I meet Nick's eyes as they twinkle amid the sparkle around us.

"Magical, right?" His typically rugged voice is low, as he tries to whisper like he doesn't want to disturb the glittering display. The effervescent sprinkles flit around us, like illuminated polka dots on our outerwear.

We are part of the light show.

"Yeah. Magic," I whisper in return.

And then, we're dancing.

With his hands on my hips, Nick bends a knee between my legs, and we sway to the sound of "Christmas Time Is Here" which isn't really a dance song. Yet, Nick has just turned it into one. Or maybe it's our surroundings of fragrant evergreens and tiny lights speckling the branches. Or maybe it's just something special in the wintery air.

Nick takes my hand and twirls me away from him before pulling me back to his chest. I spin and slip my hands up his shoulders as we slowly rotate like middle school teens at a dance with too much bulk between us in our puffy jackets. Still, heat forms as I can't take my eyes off his and he's looking at me like I'm a beacon in the dark. My mitten-covered hands slide behind his neck and my fingers itch to feel his hair, curl into the strands, and then drag forward over the short beard along his jaw.

He is enchanting and I want to believe in the hope he mentioned on the drive here.

Will things get better soon for my new family of three? Will I someday no longer work for the bank? Will we feel a little more financially stable? Will I be a lot happier?

As Nick and I turn, these things shouldn't be on my mind. Hope, he'd said. I need to seek the positive.

Be the light.

I was free from Mitch and his betrayal. He didn't control me or my kids' future. I wasn't going to work at the bank forever even if I didn't know what I'd do instead. I deserved happiness.

"Hey!" The sharp call from the path to my right has Nick and I both turning our heads.

"Oh shit," Nick mumbles.

"You can't be in there." A gruff voice echoes into the trees, breaking our little bubble of bliss and the spell of momentary magic.

My arms lower from Nick's neck, contrite like a schoolgirl caught somewhere she shouldn't be. Nick grabs one of my hands, but I no longer feel his heat between our layers. Still, his grip is tight.

"Don't let go of me," he mutters. "And run."

He takes off toward the edge of the trees, opposite the pathway, and I'm quick to follow as we hop over low shrubbery and small plants, racing for the next light display which looks like an open field.

Suddenly, the lights in the field come alive as we break free of the evergreens. Hundreds of poles illuminate at their top and swirl down to the bottom, then the upbeat pulse of "Ring Christmas Bells" by Trans-Siberian Orchestra plays, and the lights beat and flash in rhythm.

"I love this song," I call out while laughing as Nick and I escape the cover of the trees and dodge through the slim poles of dancing illumination. He continues to run straight across the field counter to the lights set in long, parallel, cornstalk-like rows.

I'm not a runner, so my legs shake trying to keep pace with the longer stride of Nick. I'm giddy once again, and breathless from the exertion.

Finally, we hit a dark patch between displays, Nick pulls me back onto the walking path as if we weren't just fugitives illegally racing through a field of luminescence.

Maybe illegal and fugitive is a bit strong, but my heart hammers in my chest as Nick quickly moves us into a tunnel of brilliant and bright white lights that arch over us.

Then he stops abruptly, spins to face me, and cups my cheeks. Lowering his face, he kisses me. The first touch is a swipe against my lips, innocent yet tempting. Then he sips at my mouth, and the freshness of mint hits me. He tastes like the color green. Finally, his tongue thrusts forward, and red-hot heat consumes me as I fall against him.

The kiss is unexpected, but I don't protest. How could I resist when I haven't been kissed in over a year? When I've never been kissed like this before? From sweet to heat in sixty seconds, and we aren't cooling down as our bodies press tighter together. My insides riot, like those firefly-like lights are fluttering around in my belly. I'm lit up from the inside out, awakened from a dimness I sensed settling in me but one I don't want to darken my outlook. On life. On love. On Christmas.

Kissing Nick is the first spark of hope I've felt in a long time. I'm not empty inside. I've been . . . dormant, maybe. Waiting. Healing. But one taste of his mouth, and I'm waking up, like the lyrics of the song that played in his truck. Something vibrant and vital ignites inside me.

Nick's arm wraps around my lower back tugging me upward as our kiss continues. My hands grip his biceps.

The strong patter of racing feet thunders past us.

"Where did they go?" someone asks.

My fingers curl tighter into Nick's firm arms, holding onto him, holding onto this kiss.

"I don't know. Damn kids," another answers.

For a second, I smile against Nick's mouth, pleased to be considered a kid.

Only, Nick doesn't stop kissing me, treating me like the woman I am as he hungrily swipes his tongue against mine, swirling and twirling, like the looping lights we raced through.

Eventually, he presses a final kiss to my mouth and pulls back. Our eyes meet. The spark in his is like cool blue flames.

Nick lowers his forehead to mine as heavy footfalls rush beside us once more. My thoughts rumble as well.

That kiss. *Talk about a light show.*

Nick slowly lifts his head and looks over mine. "I think we're in the clear now." Twisting, he glances over his shoulder before shifting his entire body. He takes my hand in his again, and without a second look at me, we walk forward.

The magic of the kiss gradually dissipates as I realize Nick might have only kissed me to disguise us from our pursuers, while that kiss just took *me* to a new stratosphere.

Moving forward beneath the illuminated tunnel like we're about to enter a different dimension, my heart still flutters, colliding with a hint of melancholy.

He didn't mean to kiss me.

However, Nick lit the match of possibility. The belief in something magical. The spectacular sensation of attraction. The probability that second chances exist.

Be the light.

Suddenly, hope is shining brighter than I'd known it could.

Chapter 4

The trip through the light show doesn't take as long as I anticipated to complete, and after our toe-curling kiss I'm having trouble concentrating on the final illuminated displays anyway. Eventually, we reach the end of the spectacle, and Nick leads me back to his truck.

We don't say much. Everything in me itches to fill the silence with idle chatter, like asking him what his favorite display was or if he had a favorite Christmas song. Instead, I keep my mouth closed, my lips still burning with the imprint of his kiss.

When we finally get back to our neighborhood, Nick pulls into his driveway. As he hops out of his truck, I climb out of the passenger side, uncertain how I'd react if he touched me again like he did when we parked at the gardens. The flame he ignited might turn into an uncontrollable blaze, and that's dangerous when the kiss was only a disguise.

With my feet firmly planted on the drive, Nick scowls at me. He opens his mouth but quickly closes it and we stand in the driveway a minute staring at one another. The mystique of the brilliant light show has dimmed.

"I had a great time tonight." I pause a beat. "You were right earlier tonight. I needed a night out, so thank you."

The corner of his lip curves. "I had a good time, too."

Nick waves out his arm toward my house, and I lead the way, mentally wishing he'd invite me to his place, knowing I won't invite him into mine.

On the front stoop of my home, I open the front door and then turn to face Nick. The Christmas lights that he installed on my house are on, outlining my home in white lights. Glittering lit icicles hang from the eaves. Nick is highlighted by the bulbs around the column he wrapped with additional lights.

"Would you like to—"

"I should probably get—" he says at the same time.

We both awkwardly laugh, but sadness strikes again. I was only a substitute date, and he kissed me as a cover from being pursued.

I take a step backward, setting my foot inside the entryway. "Thanks again for tonight."

"It was my pleasure." The twinkle in his eye is like the star atop a Christmas tree and I wish the spark was for me, but I'm starting to think the gleam is something ever-present in his sharp blue eyes.

Like the elf on my shelf, pretending to watch everything but not really seeing anything.

I weakly wave as I step further into my house. Nick waits on the stoop while I close and lock the front door. As I spin and slump against the wood, I catch a glimpse of that damn flimsy elf on top of the china cabinet.

"What are you looking at?" I grumble before heading up the staircase with a kiss on my lips and confusion in my chest.

+ + +

For several days, I don't see Nick. It's probably better we don't cross paths because I'm not certain how to face my neighbor after that fake date and pretend kiss, both of which felt very real.

Snow arrives and it's in the forecast again for later this week. Nash and Eloise will be spending the upcoming weekend with Mitch, so I make a mid-week executive decision.

The kids and I are walking down the driveway between our house and Nick's when he exits his front door.

"Hey," he calls out.

"Hi, Nick," Nash eagerly calls back. "Today we're playing hooker."

"What?" Nick stills at the top of his front steps. His gaze lands on me.

"Hooky," I correct, coming up to Nash and covering his mouth with my hand although he's already spilled a different word. "Like hockey, only *hook*-ey," I emphasize.

"We're going to get a real tree," Nash adds.

After years of having a fake tree because Mitch didn't want the mess of dropping needles and watering, I've decided we should start a new tradition this year. A real tree. I want the fragrance of balsam or spruce to permeate my home.

The change is another effort to find the Christmas spirit again.

Chopping down my own tree might be slightly overambitious, but I was willing to give it a try. I found a place that helps you cut if you run out of steam. So, I called into work and checked the kids out of school for the day despite the fact they will soon be home for two weeks on winter break.

"We're going to cut it down ourselves," Nash brags causing Nick to finally move his feet and hop down his steps before walking to the driver's side of his truck.

"Really?" Nick says, glancing at me over the hood of my SUV.

Lifting my arm, I make a muscle inside my bulky winter jacket. "I think I can handle it."

I shoveled my driveway yesterday, all by my big girl self.

"You can't even cut your own grass." Regardless of the good-natured tease in his tone, the comment hits a mark. I've let him take care of me too often. Grass cutting. Light hanging.

He crosses his thick arms, as he stands between his truck and my SUV, watching me. "If you give me a half hour, I can come with you. Cut the tree for you."

"You don't need to do that." Refusing to look at him, I open the back passenger door of my SUV and help Nash up to his car seat. He settles in and buckles himself.

Nick opens the opposite back passenger door and helps Eloise inside. Rounding the vehicle, I double check that she's properly buckled herself into her seat.

Nick catches the door before I close it.

"Holliday." My name is a whisper in the cold air. The consonants and vowels rolling over his tongue, like a late-night sleigh ride over hills. There's power in the way he's said my name. His voice pleads, apologizes, and suggests a thousand other things I can't hear without them being distinctly spoken.

So, I change the subject, not wanting to give hope to possibility *and* Nick.

"You already have a tree." Squinting in the direction of his house, I envision the tree illuminated in his front window at night with multi-colored bulbs in contrast to the white lights on his house.

"I'd like to cut down a tree with you guys." He hesitates. "Unless you want it to be only a family thing."

I glance down at Eloise, who is waiting for her door to be closed.

Nash leans forward in his seat, "Can Nick come with us, Mom? Please."

Nick and I meet eyes again. The spark I typically see is dull today. His smile is weak. He looks tired, apologetic, and sheepish. "You probably work today."

"I'm off." Our gaze lingers on one another. "But I'd need you guys to come with me. I have a plow job for a local business, and then we can hit up the Christmas tree farm. I know the best one. They have a reindeer and a sleigh ride. Hot chocolate, too." His focus stays trained on me.

Whatever farm he knows sounds even better than the place I found.

"A reindeer?" Eloise questions. "A real one?"

"A real one," Nick echoes, giving her his signature wink.

"Can we go with him, Mom?" Nash whines.

"Yeah, Mom." Nick purses those lush lips that connected with mine days ago. "Can we go with Nick?"

Sweet Jesus, he's too cute with the rugged scruff and the bad boy vibe plus his red knit cap. He's only wearing a flannel shirt and a puffy black vest despite the cool temperature.

"Okay, fine." I hesitate but Eloise is quick to unbuckle herself and Nash is doing the same, pressing open his door on the other side of the SUV. "But I at least get to *try* to chop it down."

"You can do all the work." Nick's voice fills with a grin before biting the corner of his lip. My lower belly flips when he looks at me. My gaze catches on his mouth, but I quickly look away.

I will not think of him kissing me.

There will be no snow-plow innuendo. Or chopping wood comments, either.

I will keep all my smutty Santa thoughts to myself.

+ + +

Something about a man cutting down a tree is ruggedly sexy. After my measly attempt at sawing the base of the evergreen, Nick put his thick muscles to use, until the kids could cry out "Timber." Then Nick hitched the fragrant pine over his shoulder and carried . it to his truck.

The other incredibly sexy thing about Nick is how he interacts with my children. He let Nash handle the mechanisms in his truck to lift and lower the snowplow during our half-hour detour. Then he humored Eloise near the reindeer pen, taking pictures of her with the large, antlered beast in the background. He even convinced her the animal pulling Santa's sleigh gave her a wink. He promised her she was on the nice list.

"So, you never had a real tree before?" Nick asks as the kids race around wooden cutouts of faceless elves and Santa and Mrs. Claus.

"Mitch didn't like the mess." I squint as Nash sticks his head through the Mrs. Claus frame and Eloise puts her face above the Santa suit.

"At the breakfast, he looked like a prick."

I huff, slowly walking with my hands in my jacket pockets. "He used his prick to fuck someone else while we were married."

Nick stops short. His jaw tenses while his eyes narrow, hard and dark. "Motherfucker."

With a scoff, I say, "That sums it up."

Nick glances over at Nash and Eloise, who laugh as they switch places behind the wooden Christmas couple. Nick's eyes squint again, focused, concerned. "How is he with your kids?"

I shrug. "He's good enough. He attends their school activities and pushes them towards sports." The truth is, though, he's present but not overly involved. "I don't really want to bash Mitch. He made a mistake, according to him, but that mistake is now living in my old house."

Nick watches me. His expression tightens before he tensely jokes, "With a *fake* Christmas tree."

Softly, I smile. "Yep. And probably cheap plastic ornaments."

Our family collection of ornaments is in a box labeled Christmas, stored in the leaning garage behind my new home. I'll need to dig out the special ones, representing the kids over the years, but any other ornaments will need to go. If I am buying a real tree, I am buying new decorations for it. "I planned to look at ornaments in the gift shop here."

The corner of Nick's mouth hitches up. "Sounds like a good plan." He glances at Nash who calls his name from the Santa cutout. Giving Nash a chin tip, Nick addresses me, "What will you do for Christmas this year?"

"On Christmas Eve, I'll go to church with my parents and have dinner with them. Nash and Eloise are with me this year. Mitch is supposed to come over to watch the kids open their presents on Christmas morning. He'll take them in the afternoon to his place."

I'm already anticipating a lonely day, but I don't want to think about that today.

"You haven't found the *you know what*, yet, have you?" Nick lowers his voice, conspiring with me in the Santa charade.

"No luck." I shake my head, anxious because I'm running out of time. Squinting in the sunlight gleaming off the snow, I add. "Sometimes I wish presents weren't part of the holidays."

"What?" Nick mock-shrieks, lifting his hand to his cap and forcing it back on his head before swiping it forward to right it in place. "You have to have presents."

"I know and I will. For the kids."

Nick stares at me, answering a question he doesn't ask. *Who is going to give me a present this year?*

I understand the season isn't about receiving but giving, and I'll gratefully gift my children what I can, but there's a lot of pressure in gift giving. And it sucks to get shitty presents.

Mitch was the worst gift giver.

"Our second Christmas together, I'd just found out I was pregnant with Eloise and Mitch gave me a magazine subscription. He'd convinced me to stay home to be a mom and said he wanted to prepare me for sitting home all day, eating candy, and reading magazines."

"What a fucking motherfucker," Nick grumbles.

"Yeah," I sigh, unable to defend Mitch in that gift-giving decision.

"Did you want to stay home?"

Facing Nick, I slowly smile. "I did. I didn't think I was going to be a stay-at-home mom, but when Eloise was born, I didn't want to leave her all day. Mitch and I were well enough off that I could stay home then."

I'm grateful for the years I had at home with my children. With Nash now in full-day kindergarten and Eloise in third grade, I couldn't justify being home alone. Plus, I need the money. Still, the bank isn't my dream job.

"What did you do before you were a stay-at-home mom?" Nick asks.

"I was a bank teller." He already knows that's what I do now. "But I don't love the job."

"So do something else."

"Ha. It's not that easy." We start walking again as the kids run to the next wooden display of headless elves.

"Why not?"

"It's just not. I have a mortgage and two kids." I didn't want to start calling Mitch a deadbeat dad, but he was leaning in that direction. Illinois is an equitable state and I got half of everything in the divorce, including half the value of our house, that Mitch easily shelled out in order to stay there.

"I might not have kids, but I have a mortgage and I forfeited working in the family business to become a fireman. I chose me and my happiness over everything else."

"A fireman is a noble profession," I remind him. Bank telling is not glamorous.

"It is, but it wasn't exactly approved of by my family. And it didn't pay great right away either."

Nick's house is small like mine, but plenty big enough for a bachelor. If he's been with the fire department for decades, he must be at a higher paygrade. Plus, he's a captain.

"What does your family do?"

Nick glances at Nash and Eloise as they run to another cut out of elves. "It doesn't matter. What would you do if you weren't a bank teller?"

Accepting how he sweeps away an answer about himself, I say, "I always wanted to be an author."

The words tumble out before I can rein them back. As an English major in college, that had been the plan. Only inspiration for the next great American novel hadn't struck and student loans did. My dad demanded I get a real job, not one that was whimsical or involved waiting for a lucky break.

"So you write a book."

I scoff again. "Also not that easy."

"What would you write about?"

While I'd always thought I'd write something profound or philosophical, since having children, I discovered how much I adore children's books.

Instead of answering Nick, I shrug.

He stops walking and places his hands on my shoulders. "You're lying. You know what you'd write."

"How do you know I'm lying?" Defiantly, I lift my head and glare.

"Because I know if you've been bad or good, and lying is bad."

A choked laugh fills my throat at the seriousness of his tone.

"Well, lying might be bad but I wouldn't mind being on the naughty list."

Nick straightens and I freeze. *Did I really say that out loud?*

"Anyway." I clear my throat. "How about ornament shopping?" I tip my head toward the gift shop. I don't know why we're discussing a long ago dream and a suppressed passion. We're here to enjoy cutting down a tree, watching the kids laugh, and finding decorations for a new tradition in my home.

Be present.

"Hot chocolate first?" Nick questions, still watching me, accepting that I've just brushed off answering him.

"A man after my heart," I tease.

"I'm trying," Nick says, before turning for the kids and calling their names to see if they'd like a hot drink.

BE PRESENT

Chapter 5

"Tree chopping is hard work," Nick teases from the front seat of his truck as he glances in his rearview mirror. Eloise and Nash are both knocked out in the back seat. Eloise's head is tipped toward the window. Nash's mouth hangs wide open.

"It's all the fresh air." Plus, hot chocolate, a peppermint cookie, and a sleigh ride. With new ornaments wrapped in a bag at my feet and a fresh tree in the back of the truck, I smile to myself. It's been a good day.

"What do my wondering eyes see . . . is that a smile on Miss Holliday?" Nick teases.

"I smile." And my grin grows larger.

"You have a beautiful smile, but your eyes are sad sometimes."

I blink as if that might change their appearance. An apology is on the tip of my tongue, but I hold it back. Why would I apologize? Am I sad? I wasn't. Not really, just feeling alone. Although, the day has been fun, and Nick is a good man.

He clears his throat. "How'd you get a name like Holliday if you aren't a fan of Christmas?"

"I never said I wasn't a fan," I defend but laughter fills my throat. "My dad loved the season. He was like a kid when it snowed, building a fort in the yard or a sledding hill off our back deck. He loved rolling snowmen or starting impromptu snowball fights."

My voice lowers as I recall how my dad had been so fun, but work and stress age a man.

"Anyway, he wanted to name me Winter, but my mom didn't like that. They compromised on Holliday because I could be called Holli as a kid."

"Holli," Nick tries out the name on his tongue. "Hmm. I kind of like the full name better."

"Me too." I consider how my parents used my name as more like a reprimand and Mitch spoke it in a patronizing tone. My full name felt more sophisticated.

"Tell me something about Nick Santos." I shift in my seat. "I feel like we're always discussing me."

"What do you want to know?"

"Anything. Everything." I tease wiggling my brows. "Something no one else knows."

Nick shifts in his seat, fingers spreading over the steering wheel before clutching it again.

"Or not," I quickly retract.

"My life isn't really much of a mystery, I'm just private about things." His tone sounds ominous.

"About the family business?"

"Yeah." He rubs his hand over his red cap, adjusting it on his head before pushing it back in place. "It's a touchy subject this time of year."

"Meaning?" As soon as I ask, I realize I'm being intrusive when he just said he didn't like to talk about it. "You know what? Never mind." I don't need his secrets. We've had a good day and I'm not interested in pushing him for details.

I'd love to ask what his mom meant when she sounded so proud of him for being on a date. Does he not date? When I consider the woman against his front door last summer and the scene in his yard weeks later, it's probably safe to say he doesn't date. So what is he doing spending a day with me and my kids?

"Thank you," I finally say. "It was really nice of you to spend your time with us. I know the kids had a great time."

Nick inclines his head to briefly glance at me. "But what about you? Did you have a great time?"

I fight the smile pulling at my lips. "Yeah, you're okay."

His brows lift so high his cap adjusts on his head. "Just okay? I'll need to brush up. Can't be mediocre. It's either good or bad, no in between." He winks.

I'd love to be on a naughty list with him, but I tamp down the thought and melt into the fact that Nick is a nice guy, and being in that column on the list isn't always bad.

+ + +

When we return to my house, Nick unloads our Christmas pine from his truck and gives the tree trunk a fresh cut before settling it in a base I purchased at the farm. Eloise and I might have been a bit ambitious in selecting the perfect evergreen, and this one takes up more space than I'd anticipated once inside my living room.

"Good thing you don't have a fireplace," Nick comments, putting the tree in a corner of the space. He's already told me he has one.

"How will Santa get into our house without a fireplace?" Eloise suddenly asks.

Nick and I both freeze, meeting eyes and holding our breath. *Shit.*

"Well, Santa's super smart," Nick begins. "Just like he knows if you've been bad or good, he also knows if your house has a chimney or not, and actually, all houses have a chimney."

My brows hitch wondering how Nick is going to explain this one.

"Every house has heat, so it has to have a chimney, called an exhaust. Santa can squeeze his big belly down the chute to get here."

Eloise glances around the room and gazes at the thermostat. She knows it controls the heat in our house and works with the furnace in the basement.

"Will he get burned coming through the furnace?"

I close my eyes, knowing what comes next. She's going to ask if I can turn off the heat on Christmas Eve so we don't set Santa on fire.

"Actually, Santa's fluffy and cozy suit is just something he wears for social media. You know, Instagram and all that. He wears a flame-resistant suit when he's on the job." Nick winks at Eloise.

She doesn't have an Instagram account at her young age, but she knows about such a thing from her former babysitter who was a high school girl.

"Huh." Eloise doesn't sound convinced and I'm not ready for her to stop believing even if I'm struggling to find the magic in the season. I need to do better for her.

"I'm hungry," Nash interjects and I'm grateful for the shift in focus.

"I'll order a pizza." I glance up at Nick. "Would you like to stay for dinner? Consider it payment for services rendered."

His head pops up, locking eyes with me a second, before pulling his phone from his back pocket. He checks something on the screen, then glances back at me.

"I'm sorry, I can't. I have a fireman thing."

"Oh, sure. Of course." Inviting him to dinner wasn't a proposal, but an innocent offer. It's only a pizza, but I still feel silly. *A fireman thing?* Doubt ricochets through my head. He's clearly done with us this day and I don't fault him. He probably has someone who looks like a holiday singer waiting for him.

"You aren't going to help with the lights?" Nash questions Nick.

"Gotta go, buddy." He ruffles Nash's hair.

"Who's going to do it since Dad isn't here?" Nash continues, and my heart sinks. *Oh boy.*

Nick lifts his head, looking up at me once more. His eyes soften.

"My ex always hung the lights," I clarify quietly, then lift my voice higher toward Nash. "Mom's got it."

"You won't do it the same," Eloise interjects, questioning my ability to hang Christmas lights on a tree.

"Bet your mom does it better," Nick defends. I could kiss him.

But I guess that was only a one-time thing. *Maybe next year, mistletoe.*

"I'll walk you to the door." If Nick needs to leave, it's time for him to go. I'm surprisingly eager to lose myself in decorating my real Christmas tree with fresh ornaments and lights *that I hang.*

"Sorry about that." Nick pauses at the door, swiping his cap off his head and running his hand over his hair which sticks up from static electricity. "I hope I didn't mess up with Eloise."

I wave him off. "She'll be fine. You were quick on your feet."

"Years of having to explain myself."

I stare at him. What a strange thing to say?

"I had fun today," he adds.

"Me too." I smile as I reach for the doorknob and open the front door. "Have fun at your fireman thing."

A wash of chilly air swirls into the house. It's going to snow again.

"Baby, it's cold out there," I sing.

Nick gives me a warm smile. "I really want to stay."

"But you need to go." My smile grows as we play off the controversial song's lyrics. "Have fun tonight."

Nick watches me, tilting his head as if he's trying to read me, but my voice was steady, the words sincere. Why shouldn't he have fun? He's single, handsome, and ruggedly sexy.

Still, there is disappointment deep down inside me despite being grateful that Nick took time for me and my kids today. He listens when I speak. He helps me out even when I don't ask or don't want it. He's just an all-around good guy and I like him.

I want you to stay, sings through my head.

But I nod toward my living room. "I have a hot date with some light bulbs."

Nick chuckles at the wrongness of my words. "I'll see you later."

Sure he will. I force another smile and thank him again for the day. It really was fun, and I don't intend to let his exit sour the evening. The kids and I will expand our new traditions.

Mom will hang the lights on the tree.

I got this.

Chapter 6

Hours later, a subtle knock raps on my front door.

I've been sitting in my living room, admiring my Christmas tree. I did a darn good job with the five strings of lights. And after letting Nash and Eloise hang ornaments, I only did minimal rearranging, deciding it looked good enough. It's *our* tree. With pride in my heart at our oversized evergreen, I've been taking time to reflect on the year behind me.

I'm proud of myself. I got out of a marriage that collapsed. I found a job after years of not being employed. I purchased this house, small as it is, and it's mine. The kids are thriving in their new school. My parents are still alive and love me even if they occasionally disapprove of my life choices.

A second knock patters on my door and I rise, assuming only one person would be on my stoop this late.

Opening the door, Nick stands there wearing red Santa pants, complete with fluffy white cuffs around his motorcycle boots. On his upper body, he wears a black T-shirt with a set of red suspenders and a leather jacket.

"Interesting outfit," I tease.

"I told you I had a fireman thing." He pauses and lifts a bottle of wine. "Brought you something stronger than hot chocolate."

In his other hand, he holds two extra-large plastic bags each with something bulky and rectangular inside.

"Come in." Stepping back, I admire those costume-y pajama-looking pants that hug his tight backside, accentuating the fine ornamentation of his ass. Holiday elves couldn't make a more perfect decoration.

"Where are the kids?" he asks.

"Sleeping." It's after ten, and my littles will rest well tonight, especially after the day we had. Eloise only had seven questions for our elf this evening, too tired to think of more to ask him.

"Your tree looks amazing." Nick stops in the middle of my living room and admires my handiwork.

"Not bad," I agree.

Nick twists, glancing at me over his shoulder. "Take credit, Holliday. It's beautiful." His eyes don't leave my face.

"Okay," I whisper. "It's pretty." With the multi-colored lights and the array of tin ornaments and glass bulbs, it really is a lovely tree. Not to mention, the scent is heavenly.

Nick smiles. "Better."

Then, he reaches for the sacks at his feet and opens the top of one. Slowly, he pulls out a Zlot 720.

My head snaps upward, eyes meeting his, which sparkle in the dim light of my Christmas tree. I whisper in awe, "How did you find that?"

He shrugs. "I told you . . . I know a guy."

"But earlier you asked me if I'd found one?" I question.

"Just making certain you still needed this one." He lifts it higher.

With my hands clasped in front of my chest, every fiber of my being fights the urge to hug him. He's a godsend. "This *is* a Christmas miracle."

Nick's responding smile nearly blinds me. White teeth surrounded by the mix of snow and ink in his beard and cheeks that appear to be blushing. He's so attractive it almost hurts to look at him.

"Will you take a check?" I don't have four hundred dollars in cash, and I was hoping once I found the gaming system to charge the gift on a credit card, paying off the purchase later. What's that saying about not asking permission and seeking forgiveness later? Credit cards work the same way.

"Just pay me when you can," he states, brushing off my hesitation as he slips the bulky box back into the dark bag.

I hate owing people money and I'd feel better paying him now. "Let me just write a check." I turn for my kitchen. Pulling open the drawer where I keep office supplies, pens clatter and a notebook slides around. The checkbook is buried in the back.

"Holliday," Nick whispers, his voice brushing near my ear, and reminding me of how he said my name earlier today. "Pay me later."

Spinning to face him, he's so close I catch a whiff of bayberry and snow. There's something about the scent that makes me salivate while a rush of fireflies zip down my center.

He lifts his hand and brushes back my hair, curling his fingers around my ear before running his knuckles along the side of my neck. "How about that something stronger?"

"Right." He's so close I could kiss him. *Where is mistletoe when you need it?*

Schooling my overacting libido, I step left, and reach into a cabinet for wineglasses.

"Where can I put that?" He points at the gaming system, still hidden by the plastic bag.

"I'm keeping all the gifts in my bedroom, so I'll take it upstairs when I head to bed."

Our eyes meet again, and his spark as they often do. His gaze roams my body, taking in my leggings and loose-fitting sweatshirt. Somehow, I feel undressed. *I wish he was heading to bed with me.*

"What's in the second bag?" I ask as a distraction technique, while I use a wine opener and struggle to uncork the bottle.

Nick takes the bottle and corkscrew out of my hand, finishing the job.

"Something for you." He pours us each a glass of wine and hands one to me. "Also, something you should take to your bedroom. And open when you're alone."

That certainly sounds mysterious while sexy as hell and I cross my legs as I lean against my kitchen counter, hoping to quell the sudden drumming between my thighs. Nick leans his side into a cabinet as well, remaining close to me. My dark kitchen is illuminated by the soft glow of a ceramic Christmas tree with miniature lights in the center of the table.

"Sounds . . . scandalous," I tease.

Nick taps the edge of my glass with his and raises it. "It doesn't have to be." Watching me, he lifts his glass to his lips and then drinks. I stare at his Adam's apple, rolling along his throat. The silver and black of his beard dances along his neck as he swallows.

"What are we drinking to?" I ask as I bring my glass to my lips.

"A happy Holliday." My name shouldn't sound so seductive. Like he's savoring the sound of it rolling over his tongue.

As I swallow a sip of wine too quickly, I almost choke.

With his glass in hand, Nick aims it at my refrigerator. "You hung up your list."

"I did." After we shared a hot drink the day I attempted shopping, I came home and cleaned out my purse. Then I hung the list on my fridge as a reminder to do better and figure out ways to complete all the things.

Once another sip of wine coats my throat, I suggest, "Should we head to the living room?"

Nick steps back and waves for me to lead the way. We stand before my tree again, silently admiring the softness of little lights and the glint of metal ornaments and bulbous decorations.

"You already have a present underneath your tree?" His question has me glancing down at the tree skirt where a box wrapped in white and secured with a bright red bow rests beneath the lowest branches.

"What the—?"

"Has your name on it," Nick knowingly states as I lower and read my name, written almost as if with a shaky hand. Strangely, the handwriting looks like the left-handed scribble I use to answer Eloise's elf letters.

Nick lowers his hand to take my glass of wine from me.

"What did you do?" I whisper, retrieving the package and lifting it as I stand.

"Wasn't me," he playfully defends. "Must have been your elf."

I glance up at the doll dressed in red seated on top of the television cabinet, prepared to surprise Eloise and Nash with his new viewing position when they wake tomorrow morning. The silly thing couldn't possibly bring me a gift, and I skeptically glance back at Nick.

"Probably best if you open that in your bedroom, like I said. Alone. Later maybe." Nick nods toward the staircase. "It's NSFE."

"NSFE?"

"Not safe for elves."

I laugh. The large rectangle is heavy, and I shake the package.

"Oh God, you're not one of those, are you?" Nick chuckles.

"One of what?"

"A shaker. A person who shakes her gift in an attempt to guess what it is before opening the present."

I roll my lips, fighting a smile. "Guilty, I guess." I'm actually pretty good at the shaking thing, but that's from years of buying my own gifts, wrapping them up, and pretending they came from Mitch. I'd fool the kids into believing I guessed at my false surprise present.

Nick shakes his head, teasing me. "Next gift, I'll have to make too big to shake."

I laugh. "You've already done plenty." I lift the box in my hands. "You didn't need to get me something." Guilt strikes because I don't have a gift for him and I'll need to add to my list: *present for Nick.*

What could a man like him possibly need or want for Christmas, though?

"I know I didn't need to. I wanted to." Nick lifts his glass and hastily finishes his wine before setting the glass on the table. "I'm going to let you decide if you want to open that tonight or some other evening. And on that note, I really should go."

Oh, how I want to beg him to stay.

He points at the bag with the Zlot 720 before glancing at me. "Bedroom." He nods at the oversized box in my hand. "Both of these."

His gift-giving is rather mysterious, but giddiness threatens to erupt. I haven't received a gift in years. Then again, this could all be some kind of gag.

Nick shows himself to my front door and I follow, still clutching the large box. He crosses the threshold, stepping into the cold night but then turns back around, slipping his hands into the pockets of his leather jacket.

We don't speak as his eyes pin me in place. Then his gaze scans down my body and he licks his lips before leaning toward me. He reaches over the bulky box between us and brushes my hair around my ear again, running his finger along my jaw before bringing the pad of his thumb to my lower lip.

He shakes his head as though dazed and retreats once more. His voice is soft but rusty. "Night, Holliday."

"Good night." My own voice echoes his. Tender. Low.

"I hope so." He mischievously winks then hops off my stoop.

For a second, I'm frozen in place as heat rushes through my body. Like a kid on Christmas, moving in reverse, I can hardly wait to get *up*stairs.

+ + +

When I first open the box, I stare down at the light pink tissue paper before hesitantly spreading the sheets apart. A super soft-looking robe in muted pink rests within. Gingerly, I lift the folded item as if it's fragile and precious instead of cozy and sweet. The item is heavier than a typical robe and I attribute it to the thickness. But as I loosen the intricately folded material bound by the sash, something slips out the bottom of the gift.

The item lands with a soft thud, forcing me to look toward my feet. Something silky and red is wrapped around a heavier item. The delicate fabric could not have made such a thunk. Clutching the robe underneath my arm, I bend and lift the object. Unwrapping the red covering, I discover the material is indeed silky, and see-through. Edged in fluffs of white along the hem with thin spaghetti straps, the translucent negligee leaves nothing to the imagination.

"A Mrs. Claus costume?" The thought makes me blush because my mind quickly imagines Nick in his Santa pants and me in this outfit.

But it's the solid item in my hand that has my face fire-engine red. The vibrant pink toy is long and hard with lopsided bunny-ears. Cautiously, I press a button at the bottom and feel the vibrator come to life in my palm.

"Oh," sharply escapes me followed by a giggle, as if I didn't know what the button would do or what the item is for. I could be offended, but I'm not. It's been a long time since I've owned such a thing and I don't know why I didn't consider buying one for myself sooner.

Clutching all three items to my chest, I glance back into the box which has a small white card placed in the bottom. I set everything on the bed and read the message written again in handwriting like the elf sitting on my shelf downstairs wrote it.

Even moms deserve toys. Let this bring you comfort and joy.
If you need instructions, here's my number.

I stare toward the window although Nick's house isn't in sight from my bedroom. What was he thinking giving me these things? And what am I thinking, because I'm contemplating calling him.

I drop the note back into the box and stare down at the items. Gifts given to me by my next-door neighbor, who I don't really know, but wish I knew better.

Is it appropriate to accept such a gift? More importantly, is it appropriate to give them? Does he think I'm lonely? Does he consider me pathetic? Does he feel sorry for the single mom living next door to him?

As I stare at the items again—a pretty, soft robe; a racy red nighty; and a thick sex toy—I make a decision.

Hastily, I pull off my sweatshirt and remove my bra. Then I lower my leggings and underwear. Slipping into the silky negligee, my skin pebbles at the coolness of the fabric while my nipples turn to icy peaks beneath the slippery material.

I catch a glimpse of myself in the full-length mirror on my closet door. My first reaction is to laugh at the frill of white around my thighs and the flirty material exposing too much of my body.

But upon further reflection, I can't look away.

My breasts are still plump. My hips curve outward, giving me an hourglass shape. Despite the sheer material, the slivers of stretch marks marring my stomach also brands me as a mother, reminding me I gave my body to bring two beautiful children into this world. True miracles.

My thighs are a little thicker, but perfect for Santa to slip between. With that thought, I meet my eyes in the mirror, realizing the dullness that had become a too familiar reflection has been polished. My eyes sparkle, shine even. My expression softens.

I'm still alive, still desirable. I'm a gift.

Although Nick might have given me this outfit, wearing it illuminates the light inside me desperate to gleam again.

With a gentler smile at myself, I turn back for the robe, loving the contrast as it is weighty and soft, like a warm hug.

Leaving the front open, I sit on the edge of my bed, then lift the notecard once again while holding the vibrator.

Could I do this? Should I?

At the very least, I should thank Nick for his generosity. That would be the polite thing to do. Just a brief little thank you for your thoughtfulness.

With that as my excuse, I dial his number.

He answers on the second ring. "I was hoping you'd call."

"It's not too late?"

"Never." His breathy response has me closing my eyes, shoring up courage to say what I'm about to say.

"Thank you. Your gifts were . . . generous."

"I didn't offend you, did I?"

"No." My lids spring open, and I stare down at the magic wand I hold in my hand. My core pulses. My legs clench.

"Does everything fit?" The question is innocent enough. A hope that the correct size was purchased. Still, I have no idea how my new toy will feel.

"I've only tried two of the three items, but those both fit perfectly."

Nick hums through the phone. "Should we see how the last item works out for you?"

I don't answer at first as I fall to my back on the bed and cross my legs, attempting to squelch the throbbing between them until I can get off my phone.

"I'm not sure—"

"I'm glad you called. I forgot to include the instruction manual."

I giggle, anxious and giddy. "I think I can figure it out."

"But maybe you need me to interpret the directions. They're in six different languages." I hear the smile in his voice. "You can take your pick."

"Do you know six different languages?"

"No. Only four."

My brows lift at the playfulness in his voice.

"What am I doing?" I whisper, with my legs crossed tightly, but desperate to be spread and use my new toy.

"You're letting me instruct you." His tone turns firmer. The edge sharper, almost commanding, and God, I want him to command me.

"You said you wanted to be a little naughty. I thought I could help you make the list."

"This is crazy," I mutter, hardly louder than the squeak of a mouse.

"Holliday." The determination in his voice has me holding my breath. "Lie back on your bed."

"I already am," I admit.

"Good girl."

"I thought you were helping me be bad," I tease while a rush of excitement whirls up my middle.

"Spread your legs."

Yep, that does it for me. I scoot up the bed and separate my thighs.

"What are you wearing?"

I almost laugh at the seriousness of his question. "Both the robe and the nighty."

He hums again with my answer. "Why both?"

"I like how the silkiness feels sexy while the softness of the robe is comforting."

"God, I'd like to feel them on you."

I stare up at the ceiling, wondering if he's serious. I could invite him over, but it's late and I don't think that's the purpose of tonight.

"Holliday, honey, instruction one says to spread your legs."

"Already there." My center pulses wickedly as my knees fall open.

"Step two. Turn on the toy. Batteries included."

I bite my lip, but I do as instructed, listening to the tender vibration as the instrument pulses.

"Step three—"

"How many steps are there?" My breath rushes.

"Eager?" he teases, his chuckle deep and jovial.

He has no idea. If I don't get this thing lowered and against sensitive skin, I might combust. Good thing he's a fireman because I'm ready to go up in flames.

"Step three." He pauses. "Insert into your pussy. Place the small rabbit ear at your clit. Let me hear you."

"Is that final step really part of the directions?"

"Yes," he groans.

And I match the heaviness in his throat with my own moan that fills the phone as I place the toy between my thighs and easily slip it inward.

Slowly. Filling. Satisfying. My breath hitches with each thought.

"Jesus," he hisses. "Tell me what it feels like."

"Another instruction?" I choke around my sassiness as the vibrator hums inside me and against me. I close my knees, intensifying the rush. "Oh God."

"That's it, honey. Let me hear how good it feels to be a little bad."

I purr and roll my head to the side as my body comes undone. I'm lighting up like a Christmas tree.

"Tell me something." Nick moans into the phone. "Are you thinking of me? Are you wishing I was over there right now?"

"Oh God," I whimper afraid to admit the truth.

"Think of my fingers inside you. My thumb on your clit. I bet you're soaked."

"Urgh," I grunt.

His voice.

The thought.

I'm going to come so fast.

"I have my hand around my dick, Holliday, and you know what I'm thinking of?"

"Tell me," I whisper, then I nearly beg. "Tell. Me."

"Your hot pussy slicking my dick and then I'm—"

"Ahhh," I cut him off as the rapid rush of release rips through me like the swiftness of an out-of-control sled sailing off a jump. I'm catching heat despite the chill on my skin, and then I'm soaring.

"Nick," I groan as I clutch at the phone in one hand and the toy between my legs with the other, giving into the naughtiest thing I've ever done.

My neighbor phone-talked me through an orgasm.

"Holliday." His voice hitches, catching as it does as he rounds over my name. He grunts once. Then "Fuuck!"

Silence fills the phone, and my imagination takes me next-door, where he's clutching at himself, thinking of me, as the rush hits him.

A minute passes before Nick blows out a breath. "Feel better?" he mutters, smokey and satisfied himself.

My only response is to mimic his hums.

"It occurred to me we didn't have each other's number and I figured it's time we shared them. It's one reason I haven't called you the past couple of days."

I snort as I roll to my side, turning off the vibrator and momentarily tossing it on the bed. "If this is how you pass out your number . . ." I don't want to think about him generously giving out pretty robes and slinky nighties to women everywhere.

"Actually, I just wanted to give you a gift. And to get *your* number."

"Why?"

"Tis the season. And I want to change your mind about gifting presents. Doesn't it feel wonderful to receive one?" His laughter is full of flirtation and afterglow—if a burly man can glow.

"One should never expect a gift, though." I sound like my mother and the thought pricks the euphoria of what we just did. I drop my voice and whisper, "But thank you." I am grateful. His present might have been one of the most thoughtful gifts I've ever received.

"I was wondering if you'd go somewhere with me."

My mind flips back to the holiday light show. The night was magical. Maybe that kiss meant something to him after all? A woman can dream.

"Where?" I tuck my knees up to my chest and pull the long length of my new robe over them.

"It's a fundraiser. A party a few firehouses put on for a fellow firefighter. It's holiday themed. A costume party, actually."

"By costume, do you mean I should wear the gift you gave me? It hints a little at Mrs. Claus."

"I doubt the big man's wife wears such an outfit, and that gift was for your eyes only, unless you ever want to share it with me."

My gaze flits to the window, even knowing I can't see his house from my vantage point, but curious all the same, if he wants to see me wearing the luxurious gift he gave me.

"Come with me, Holliday."

The teenager in me wants to tell him I already did. Instead, I say, "I don't know what I'd wear. What do people dress up as for a Christmas costume party?"

"Lots of variations of Santas as most of us have that outfit already. Elves. Some angels. But it's all up for interpretation. You can wear white, wrap yourself in red ribbon, and call yourself a peppermint stick for all I care."

Would he offer to lick me if I did? I don't dare ask.

"Okay." My answer is soft. I'm sleepy and warm. "I'd love to go with you to the party."

"I forgot to ask about the kids. Would this work?"

"Mitch has the kids this weekend."

Silence falls between us again and I can't decipher if the quiet is heavy or speculative. Where would a date lead this time? Is this actually a date, or am I just accompanying him to a fundraiser?

"Then you'll go with me?"

I want to read hopefulness in his question, but I won't project my feelings onto him. "*Then* I'd love to attend."

"Friday at seven. It's a date."

Chapter 7

When Nick picks me up, he's creatively dressed like a badass Santa, complete with his red velvet pants with white fluffy cuffs, but the suspenders and the tight white Henley make me want to ask to sit on his lap and tell him everything I want.

"A snow woman?" He questions, hitching a brow at my not-quite-so-original outfit, in which I'm wearing a white dress that might be a bit summery for a winter affair, along with a green scarf around my neck and black combat boots I found in the back of my closet. I'm also wearing throwback white tights, and a magician's top hat from Nash's stash of dress-up clothes. I've even dabbed orange face paint on the tip of my nose, like it's a carrot.

"That would be Freya the Snowwoman to you." I pull at the side of my dress and bend my knee for a swift curtsy.

"You look more like a tempting snowball."

I have no idea if that's a compliment, so I motion to the bushy clump of leaves with white berries in his hands. "Are those for me?"

"Mistletoe." He holds the bunch upward. It's real greenery, not a plastic imitation.

"Thank you." I reach for the delicate plant but Nick lifts it upward. He taps his cheek, innocently suggesting he's due a kiss.

Laughing, I place my hands chastely on his shoulders and tip upward, pressing a kiss to the corner of his mouth.

Relief washes over me that there isn't awkward tension or bashful eye-avoidance after what we'd done the other night. It's almost as if it never happened. Nick didn't call me the next day. Then again, I didn't call him. A simple text from him confirmed our plans this evening, thoughtfully double-checking that the kids were taken care of for the night. However, the silence between us had me overthinking this evening.

It's only a fundraiser, I'd often remind myself.

"So where exactly are we going tonight?" I ask as I reach for my coat draped over the back of a chair. Nick takes the coat from me and hands me the mistletoe. While he holds open my jacket, I stare at him. I can't remember the last time someone held my coat to help me slip it on. The gentlemanly behavior seems so antiquated and yet I'm tickled pink by the gesture.

Once my coat is on, Nick motions his head toward the mistletoe in my hand. "Might want to leave that here. It'd be dangerous to bring it with you."

"All the boys will want to kiss me?" I tease, wiggling the green bunch at him like its magic or something.

"Probably. Then I'd get into a fight, and we'd be kicked out of the party." He winks. "But let's add, I'd want to kiss you myself, and then we'd miss the party."

He bites his lower lip, eyes roaming my outfit again.

He hasn't kissed me yet, though. Not a real kiss. Not a kiss that wasn't camouflage from security.

While I'd love to tell him he can kiss me, and we can skip the festivities tonight, it's probably better if we leave before I do something that foolish.

+ + +

"You didn't answer me. Where are we going?"

"Like I said on the phone, it's a fundraiser called A Snowball's Chance. It's a play on snowballs not having a chance in hell. We're fireman, so hell is our domain. Get it?"

Understanding, I smile.

"Anyway. Zebb is a fellow fireman and one of my good friends, and his little girl has some serious medical needs. He has a ton of money as a former NFL player, but he and a friend developed an organization called Snowball's Chance to provide help for families with children who have severe medical needs and struggle with the steep costs. Zebb is a great guy, and his daughter Tam is a hoot."

The animation in Nick's voice has my brows lifting. He's proud to be a part of this organization in some way.

"A few firehouses come together to host this event, each chipping in for the party, but also collecting funds for the cause. Last year we raised close to twenty-thousand dollars. The bar comps all the drinks and firefighters like to drink."

"I feel bad. I didn't bring much cash to donate."

Nick scowls at me. "You don't need to donate. I already purchased our tickets."

"Still, 'tis the season." I haven't done anything to donate food or gifts this year. When I was married to Mitch, I'd purchase additional gifts from giving trees and schoolkid wish-lists, but there aren't extra funds this December.

I haven't even paid Nick for the Zlot 720 yet.

Nick gives me a quick glance as he weaves through side streets leading us further into the city of Chicago.

"You know it isn't always about money. Give where you can, however you can. Sometimes that means giving time instead of food or cash."

"Like you volunteer at places dressed like a hot Santa."

Nick shrugs. "That doesn't really count. I like playing Santa. The smile on kids' faces. The excitement of the season. But my part is easy. The real deal is a tougher job." He chuckles. "And did you just say I was hot?"

"You know you are," I tease, waving up and down at him. "You've got the whole sexy Santa thing going and those come-sit-on-my-lap eyes."

Nick's head turns quickly, wide-eyed for a second before returning his attention to the road. "If I asked you to sit on my lap, would you?"

I bite my lower lip, fighting a smile. "Depends on if you've been bad or good this year."

Nick barks out a laugh. "Oh, I've been a very, very bad boy." His fingers clutch tighter at the steering wheel as he expertly guides us down a major street.

I don't dare ask how bad or with whom. My imagination already pictures Nick in a hundred positions doing an equal number of graphic things with his lips, his tongue, and his fingers.

"But back to the donation stuff for a second," he says, breaking the mood as he flips on his blinker and slows to parallel park. "Go to a shelter where they serve dinner or volunteer for a night ministry where they pack food bags to pass out to homeless people."

I'd have to think about it, but I understood what Nick was saying. There are other ways to be generous. Time was one of them.

Like being present. Or a light of hope.

I'd amend my list.

Donate time.

+ + +

Murphy's Bar was a Chicago staple. Like many bars that have been around for decades, it was long and narrow with dark paneling and few windows. Positioned on a corner, the locals might consider it a neighborhood hot spot. A line of people wanting general admission stood outside the entrance. Tickets for the event were collected at the door. The place is packed, chaotic, and loud.

Nick easily ushers us inside and we squeeze our way through the crowd. The bar is garishly decorated with tinsel and holiday lights. Still, it's festive with silver and gold foiled streamers and multi-colored bulbs on anything that will hold them.

"What would you like?" Nick shouts over the riotous rendition of a Christmas song people are singing to off-key and without a care. I can't help but smile.

"I'll have a glass of red wine," I shout back. "Malbec, if they have it."

While Nick has wedged himself between two guys, clapping one on the back to place our order, a man on the other side of him shifts and levels me with an intense stare. He's a large guy, broad across the shoulders and firm in the middle, although I can't gauge his height as he's seated on a stool. With hair a mix of snow and ink, he's a solid silver fox. However, he looks like he's been at the party before it was a party.

"Hey, snowball." He smiles at me.

I open my mouth to greet him, but Nick responds. "Hey, Brock. Good to see you." He holds out a hand and Brock shakes.

"You, too," Brock offers. "But who is Feisty?" His gaze fixes on me.

"You mean Frosty," I correct, although I'd called myself Freya earlier.

He slowly smiles. I bet women drop their panties for that smirk.

"Not a thing cold about you, girl," he adds.

Nick wraps an arm around my shoulder. "This is my neighbor, Holliday."

"No shit." Brock's forehead furrows.

"No shit," I reply, trying to shake off the blasé label of being Nick's neighbor.

Brock's eyes narrow to slits and he smiles wide. Pointing a finger at me, he says, "I like this girl." Only it comes out like one word. *Izlikethisghaul.*

"Where's Zebb?" Nick asks, looking over heads for someone.

"He's late." Brock rolls his eyes. "Probably making out in the car with his wife."

I glance up at Nick puzzled, but he shakes his head.

Hands double tap on the bar. "Okay. Fireball for the snowball," Brock announces to the bartender. "New initiate." He hitches a thumb at me.

"Oh, I don't need—"

"Snowball's Chance, snowball. Gotta prove you can handle the heat," he says to me. "How naughty you gonna be tonight?"

I glance up at Nick, who shakes his head again like I should just ignore this Brock character. But something about Nick calling me his neighbor doesn't settle well with me. "Give me the damn shot."

Brock whoops and slaps the bar once. "Now that's what I'm talking about."

A shot glass filled with amber liquid appears on the counter, and I drink like I'm a sorority-girl when I haven't done hard alcohol in more than a decade. The burn going down is fire and spice, and my insides instantly warm.

"Gonna melt you, snow lady," Brock teases, turning toward me.

"That's a hundred bucks," the bartender yells and my eyes widen. *Holy shit.* I don't have a hundred dollars on me.

Brock is already pulling a bill from his wallet. Nick is faster, slapping the hundred on the bar. "Now stop hitting on my date."

Brock narrows his eyes, tilting his head. "You said she was your neighbor."

I chew at my lower lip. I might like this Brock guy after all. Although if this is his idea of flirting, it's a strange way to hit on a woman.

"I'm sorry about that," I say to Nick. "I'll pay you back."

"It's all for a good cause." He doesn't even blink that he just paid one-hundred dollars for a shot he hadn't ordered me. "But let's get you away from him." He tips his head at Brock.

Brock scowls at Nick. "When you're ready to dump Santa, come find my lap."

"Dude," Nick growls before Brock turns back toward the bar.

We wait for my wine and Nick's beer and then press through the crowd toward a high-top table along the wall. Men and women come and go, recognizing Nick, wishing him happy holidays, or discussing some familiar event. Nick introduces me, but I generally stay quiet as I don't know anyone.

It's a good reminder of what dates might be like if I ever considered going on one in the future. For now, I'm just the neighbor out with the guy next door. With that in mind, I take a hefty sip of my wine.

When a couple enters dressed like an angel and Father Christmas, loud cheers erupt.

"That's Zebb. Snowball's Chance is his foundation." Nick tips his head toward the couple about our age. They both have brown hair while Zebb's is speckled with gray. Scruff decorates his jaw, and he has a smile like an angel's, although he's wearing a dark green robe and a holly wreath on his head. He's extremely good looking and his wife is equally beautiful in a sexy angel costume with giant wings that keep swatting people. She laughs at something Brock says and waves her hand to dismiss the bartender.

They make their way through the crowd until they get to us.

"Nick." Zebb holds out a hand, enthusiastic to see my neighbor, and they hug like old friends. "You remember Eva."

Her name is pronounced like Evan without the n. It's so pretty.

"Hey, Nick." She steps up to him, giving him a quick hug while Nick kisses her cheek.

"Guys, this is Holliday."

Zebb's head turns first. "The hot neighbor?"

Heat rushes over my cheeks and I catch a glance with Eva. She quickly says, "I love your costume. Better than all the elf-wannabees."

"I've noticed." We share a smile about the number of women dressed like sexy elves, possibly hoping to be willing 'helpers' to the various Santas tonight. As I've had time to look around while Nick greets people, the place is like a Santa convention.

"So, what do you do?" Eva asks me.

Over a certain age, it's difficult to make new friends. I'd lost many of the people I thought were my friends during the divorce. The neighborhood Karens, and Kathys, and Heathers, all stayed in the suburbs while I was booted to the city. From my old community, you didn't cross a certain avenue heading south without having a strong misconception that you've entered the 'hood.

"I work as a bank teller." I expect the conversation to end there, but Eva becomes a chatterbox about banks and the holidays. How people give cash as a gift when they don't know what to purchase someone. She then goes on to explain how she used to work for Ashford's, a major department store in downtown

Chicago, and now owns her own boutique shop near Roscoe Village.

"Come in sometime. I'll give you the friends and family discount." Her smile assures me her offer is genuine, even though we've just met.

"Do you have any children?" she asks next, which leads to me explaining Eloise and Nash, and Eva talking about Tam.

"She's Zebb's daughter." Eva looks up at her husband. "But I'm adopting her."

"That's so wonderful." It's inspiring actually and I reach for her wrist as a means to express my admiration. Plus, the wine is going to my head which always makes me overly affectionate.

"Another round?" Zebb asks as our party seems to suddenly be four.

"Malbec." I lift my glass.

Nick raises his beer and Zebb waves a hand to signal to the bartender.

"Want a Coke or something?" Zebb asks his wife with concern.

"I'm okay with lemon water." She lifts the glass and takes a sip meeting my eyes.

I know that look. "Are you—"

"Let's dance." Eva grabs my arm and tugs me toward a mash of people in a corner as there isn't an official dance floor. A disc jockey spins more Christmas tunes that the crowd continues to belt out loud and proud like they're attending a rock concert.

"I'm sorry," I blurt as we join the mayhem.

Eva places a finger over her lips. A warning that Zebb might not know yet, and it's going to be a surprise.

For a second, I miss the possibility of having another baby. After Eloise and Nash, I would have had another child, but Mitch

91

didn't want more. I was happy with two, felt fortunate even, and didn't give it another thought. But moments like this, learning someone is pregnant, brings the longing back.

Quickly, I snap out of baby-funk and into the craziness of singing Christmas carols like rock ballads while dancing to them.

"I haven't danced in years," I confess to Eva.

"It feels good to let loose once in a while."

When *was* the last time I really let loose? The memory of a few nights ago comes back to me and I seek Nick among the crowd. I don't have to look far because he's made it to the edge of the makeshift dance area with Zebb. Both men are watching us.

"It's almost unfair how hot fireman are," I say.

"Pun intended," Eva laughs.

"Who is the guy at the bar? The one trying to get everyone to drink Fireball shots."

"That's Brock, Zebb's brother." Eva rolls her eyes. "He's harmless but a real Grinch. He hates Christmas." Eva giggles. "Then again, I used to, too."

"I'm struggling with it myself this year."

Eva nods as if she understands. "It happens. The holidays are so overwhelming. The pressure. The packages. The family. The frenzy." She waves her hands around her head. "But this year, I'm loving all of it."

Being that she's newly married to Zebb and adopting his daughter, plus secretly pregnant, there is much to be excited about.

"I need to get back to that feeling. Of loving the holidays."

Eva glances back in the direction of Zebb and Nick. "Maybe you'll get your own Father Christmas, like a fairy godmother, only sexy and in a Santa suit."

I glance at Nick as well and laugh. "Maybe."

The song shifts to "Christmas Time Is Here" and the dance space clears a bit as people take a breather with the slower melody. I watch as Nick sets his beer down on a table and stalks toward me.

"They're playing our song," he says, wrapping an arm around my waist and tugging me against him.

I catch myself on his chest and shakily laugh. "Our song?" Instantly, I remember dancing under the lights at the Botanic Garden. While the bar's ceiling is covered in blinking Christmas lights, it's not quite the same as evergreens and firefly-like dots.

Nick lowers his head and takes one of my hands in his. With my other hand still on his chest and his arm around my back, he dangles our joined hands along our sides.

"I feel like I've hardly spoken to you tonight. And I want to punch Brock for flirting with you."

I snort. "Easy there, Santa. Don't want to suddenly make the bad-boy list. And I don't think buying me a shot was flirting. Plus, you're a popular guy. You seem to know everyone."

"It's just the CFD." *Chicago Fire Department.* "We're a huge family."

"Must be nice. I'm only the neighbor." I don't intend to say it as loud as I do, but Nick stills. His heavy brows pinching, suggesting he heard me.

"Why would you say that?"

My mouth pops open ready to explain myself but what can I say? The neighbor is who I am to him. I'm the one with foolish hopes of wanting more. And my response was snarky honesty. I'm envious of this fireperson community. For just a moment, I miss my old neighborhood.

He presses, "Do you think that's all you are to me?"

"That's how you introduced me. It's no big deal—" I lose my train of thought when he gently pinches my chin.

His eyes search mine, deep and questioning. "What do you think the other night was?"

"I . . . I don't know." A lonely woman responding to a generous gift that the smexy man next door offered her.

"You have no idea how tempting you are, do you?"

My brows lift. "Well, I am the *hot* neighbor," I anxiously tease using Zebb's words and what Nick's mother almost called me when he phoned her on our way to the light festival.

Nick chuckles. "Jesus, I'm not doing a good job here if you don't get it." With my hand already in his, Nick leads me back toward our table where I'd left my jacket. Without breaking hold of my hand, he swipes up my long coat and leads us toward the entrance, only he veers hard left and presses through an exterior door. The cold night immediately hits me as we stumble onto an enclosed patio.

"Put this on." Nick releases my hand and holds out my jacket. After the heat of the bar, the night air feels refreshing but I won't last long out here without my winter coat. Slipping my arms inside the heavy material, I turn to face Nick.

His hands cup my jaw. Then he's kissing me.

The warmth of his lips keeps the combustible flame inside me on a high burn. His tongue crosses the seam of my lips, and that flame becomes an inferno. His mouth is hot and eager like he kissed me beneath the light tunnel when we ran from security. Only, we aren't being chased tonight. We aren't hiding in a kiss to disguise ourselves. This is pure passion on the outdoor patio of a city bar underneath a dark December sky.

Nick breaks first. "I've been wanting to do that since the first time."

"Why didn't you?" I ask, sheepishly glancing up at him.

"I don't know." A crease forms between his brows like he really doesn't have an answer. "Thank goodness I bought you mistletoe."

His mouth crashes mine again, not needing the plant as an excuse to kiss me. My fingers clutch his shirt while his hands move to my hair, fisting in the long length.

"You have no idea what I want to do to you," he growls before kissing me harder, his tongue thrusting deeper.

I didn't think any kiss could top the first one he gave me, but this one has my toes curling in my boots and my fingers tugging his Henley. He isn't close enough.

"What do you want to do?" I finally mutter as we take a breath.

"Naughty things. Very naughty things."

Chewing on my lower lip, I glance at him. "Like what?"

"Snowball," he sighs, stealing Brock's nickname. "You look angelic and innocent, and I'm the damn devil who wants to muddy you up."

Yes, please.

"Nick." His name is a desperate plea before his mouth is back on mine, kissing me with hungry lips and savoring licks. He moves to my neck, tugging on the scarf around it. I can't seem to get it off fast enough. I'm choking on the flannel wrap, desperate for him to get to my skin.

Once his mouth meets my flesh, he sucks at a spot that triggers a rush of pleasure straight down my middle, like the rapid melting of snow. Or the rising flame of a wildfire.

Next, Nick presses off my jacket. "Put this on backward."

I don't understand what he means, until he spins me so my back hits his front. The inside of my coat covers my chest. Nick lifts my wrists to hold me steady against the brick wall I suddenly face. The heat of his body behind me is its own comforting wrap, keeping me warm as his hands skim around my waist and fist at my dress.

"Talking you through the other night. Listening to your soft hums and sharp breaths. God, I just wanted to be in the room and watch you like that damn elf on your shelf."

I laugh at the sudden reference to the childish toy in my house.

"Only what I want to do to you is not safe for elves."

Slowly, my dress is being dragged up my thighs, bunching toward my hip.

"Let me feel how hot you are, neighbor." Tease and seduction in his voice fills my ear, stealing the oxygen in my lungs.

"That's *hot* neighbor to you," I joke breathlessly.

He nips hard at the juncture of my neck and shoulder. "You're *my* neighbor," he preens. "I want you all to myself."

Well.

"Say yes, Holliday." His fingers are underneath my dress and caressing the front edge of my hip, tempting me with how close he is to a sacred spot.

"Yes," I exhale. *Please, baby Jesus and all the saints in heaven, let this man touch me.*

Nick's hand slides forward, cupping me over my tights. He hisses. "Sizzling."

I'd laugh if it didn't sound so damn accurate.

"I want you to melt, snow lady." He breathes into my neck. "And make a puddle against my fingers." He licks along the column of my throat.

"Please," I whimper. It's been more than a year since I've been touched by someone else.

Nick moves his hand to dip into my tights and underwear, rushing over the mound and against sensitive folds. My knees give out again and I press my head momentarily to the cold brick before me.

Nick groans as his fingers dive into slick heat, dipping in until they can't go any further. When he pulls back, I whimper, desperate for him to stay within my body. He doesn't disappoint, filling me again and again before dragging to the edge and teasing my clit.

My head falls back to his shoulder, and I hum.

"There she is," he murmurs, seductive and sweet. "You're more fire than ice, honey. And I want to be the one to make you burn."

With the attention he's giving the sensitive nub, it isn't going to take long. My breath hitches. My legs stiffen.

"Almost there, aren't you? I can feel it. Hear it. Dammit, I want to taste you."

He leaves my clit and dips two fingers into me again. I cry out, but he's quickly back on point, driving me higher and higher with his thumb teasing me.

My hands fist against the wall. "Nick," I groan.

"That's right. Call my name. Now be a good girl and come for me. Let me feel how much you want me."

Dammit. I do want him. And while I want this orgasm, it isn't going to be enough.

Still, my insides overheat and my legs quiver. I'm practically clawing at the brick wall when I finally give in and melt over his fingers like he asked. I'm a puddle, dripping and draining, and collapsing forward, but Nick keeps me upright, until the last drop.

Pressing my forehead to the wall, my breathing is as ragged and rough as the texture of the brick.

"Damn, Holliday," he mutters against my neck before slowly dragging his fingers from my tights. He spins me to face him and kisses me lightly, sweetly, before releasing me and lifting his hand, making me watch him suck on his fingers. "Better than peppermint sticks."

Shaky and rough, laughter clogs my throat. I can't believe I just let him finger me on a bar patio, against a brick wall.

"I'd love nothing more than to take you to my truck and take this to a new level, but it's fucking freezing out here."

My gaze lowers to his Henley. He wasn't wearing a jacket when he picked me up. All he has on is this underlayer shirt; however, my scarf is around his neck. Somewhere I've lost Nash's magician hat, plus my jacket is on backward. The weather really isn't conducive to truck sex.

"Thank you," I whisper, meeting his eyes that are almost coal in color but dance with mirth.

"For what?"

"For helping me be naughty."

Nick chuckles and tugs me to him. "Honey, you're still too good for me, but I'm not ready to give you up." He pulls back so I look up at him. "And you aren't just the neighbor. Even the hot neighbor. You're *my* neighbor and that's all that matters."

Like a Christmas miracle, snow begins to fall around us like a damn fairy tale, dusting us in light fluffy flakes of white. We both look up, blinking at the slow onslaught.

"It's so beautiful," I marvel. "Like being in a snow globe." I swallow around sudden thickness in my throat, remembering how we danced among the dark evergreens and the soft fluttering lights felt like a snow globe then as well. "If only we could freeze time." I'd freeze this moment for all of eternity because I'd love to claim Nick as mine.

Dear Santa, can I keep him?

Chapter 8

We returned to the party where I celebrated life like I was twenty, not forty.

Afterward, with Nick's support, I made it to my bedroom where he tucked me in without undressing me or making any advances.

"Did you have fun?" he asked, brushing back my hair once I collapsed on my bed.

"The most fun," I whispered, before admitting a truth I hadn't been willing to face. "I felt like me again."

I missed being easygoing and a little reckless. And I did enjoy the raunchy round of Jingle *Balls* and a second shot of Fireball.

For a few hours, the holiday spirit warmed my insides but that could have also been the endless kisses Nick gave me in front of his friends and coworkers. He never let go of my hand or my hip. He played with my hair and caressed my neck, and I felt . . . desired . . . from all the attention. I'd missed these kinds of simple, affectionate touches, and I craved Nick's.

As morning dawns, though, I'm embarrassed by how much holiday cheer I consumed. I haven't been hungover since sometime in the early two-thousands which isn't saying much. I'm a lightweight. And I owe Nick an apology.

While I linger in bed, I shoot off a quick text.

I overdid the holiday spirit last night and I'm sorry.

His response is quick. **Not a thing to apologize for, snowball. Or should I call you Fireball now?**

Ha Ha. Chewing at my lip, I type out: **Are you home?**

Had the day shift. Twelve hours on. Be home later tonight.

I nod as if he can see me and hesitate. Will we see each other again soon? Is it too forward to ask? This is why I can't date yet. I don't know how these things work and I don't have the emotional energy.

My focus for now needs to be Christmas. I have just over a week before the official day hits and my list is still incomplete.

One additional thing I need to find is a neighborly gift for the man next door.

+ + +

After the hustle and bustle of shopping in stores cramped with stressed-out shoppers, I believe I have something perfect for my neighbor. It isn't much. Just a token of my affection and appreciation for all he's done for me this season. Well, actually since I moved in next-door.

With the kids gone for another night, I attempt to settle into a few holiday movies, but find frustration in every happily ever after. Eventually, I take a bath, soaking in the tub like I had weeks ago. I'm almost as restless now as I was then. When I finally step out, wrapped in the robe Nick gave me and check his driveway for his truck, I admonish myself and turn on a Christmas classic for mindless entertainment.

Eventually, I need something for dinner, but stall before opening the fridge. My list hangs beneath a magnet.

Buy presents. Be present.
Wrap gifts. Wrap someone in a hug.
Send gifts. Send Peace.
Shop for food. Donate food.
Make cookies. Make love.
See the lights. Be the light.

Have I done any of these things? So far it felt like Nick had done them *for me*. He'd been present when we went to chop down a Christmas tree. He'd been the light the night he took me to see the garden show. And he financially donated to a worthy cause and physically played dress-up Santa at breakfasts.

Disappointment hits me. I'm not fulfilling my list. I'm failing once again, and I rip the slim sheet from the magnet, tear it in half, and toss it in the trash.

"There's always next year," I mutter, a saying famous for any Chicago Cubs or Bears fan. But the holiday isn't a sport, and I'm not winning at it anyway.

Skipping dinner, I reach for the bottle of red on my counter and return to my living room as headlights scan across the window and lead up the drive Nick and I share.

My heart hammers. *He's home.*

Looking down at myself and glancing at the bottle of wine in hand, an idea forms in my head. Probably not *exactly* the intention where the list was modified, but it's still an item on the list.

Make love.

I rush to my room to change my clothes.

+ + +

Standing on Nick's front stoop, I shake out my hand, spreading my fingers before clenching them into a fist.

"It's just a neighborly visit," I tell myself. "I'm returning the favor." He'd paid one-hundred dollars for a shot last night. The least I can do is offer him a bottle of wine. Wiggling my legs, I continue muttering to myself. "As a thank you."

Tipping back my head, I stare up at the sky, heavy with the scent of snow. "And now I'm talking to myself."

I lower my head, face Nick's door, and lift my fist to knock. The sharp rap shouldn't startle me. I'm the one knocking after all, but I flinch, then giggle, as I disturb the peacefulness of a silent night on our street.

I knock a second time. "If he doesn't answer in sixty seconds, I'll go back home." I'll pop this bottle of wine, retrieve my generous gift from Nick and take care of myself. I might even let that damn elf watch. Give him something to report to the man in red.

My breath mists in the cold night as I exhale and hang my head. Thoughts of Nick inside with someone else cross my mind. It's possible and it hurts to consider.

Magical garden lights and a fundraising party do not make us a couple. We aren't dating or officially anything other than neighbors.

The truth stings more than I like.

This is ridiculous. Turning on my heels, I prepare to leave his stoop when the front door flings open. Nick stands just inside. His feet bare. His hair damp. A tight tee covers his abs, but his jeans are low-slung and not completely buttoned as if he just tugged them on.

"Holliday?" His voice registers surprise while his eyes roam down my body, taking in my long jacket, my bare legs, and the impractical heels on my feet.

"You once mentioned your fireplace. I thought I'd have a look at how cozy it is." My head is held high as one of the worst pickup lines tumbles from my mouth.

Nick's lips slowly curl, and he steps back. "Yes. Let's check out my fireplace."

Once I step over the threshold, he closes the door behind me. "Can I take your jacket?"

"Not yet," I say, using my coat as a shield. *What am I even doing?* "It's chilly out there. Let me warm up a bit."

Nick watches me, almost silently questioning: isn't that what the fireplace will be for?

Still, he points me toward his living room. His home mirrors mine. The entry leads down a hallway to the kitchen. A partial wall offers the living room privacy from the hall. The fireplace is a focal point. Nick has a leather couch facing the open hearth with a flat screen over the mantel. A wooden chair sits in the corner near the front window, like a punishment seat or a place someone might read a book to children sitting on the floor. The furnishings are completely opposite from one another.

A Christmas tree fills another corner. Colorful lights illuminate the fresh evergreen, and ornaments in various shapes and sizes hang from what looks like a professionally decorated tree.

"Your tree is so beautiful." The balsam fragrance is nearly intoxicating.

Nick steps toward the fireplace and flicks a switch, igniting a low flame. Soft flames crackle over the logs inside his fireplace. With the muted lights of his tree and the warm blaze, the room is cozy, romantic even.

And the hum beneath my skin won't seem to settle, neither will the nervous chill running over my flesh.

Nick gestures to the couch, before saying, "I'll be right back with some glasses."

When he disappears into his kitchen, I step toward the built-in bookcases on either side of his fireplace, admiring a collection of well-worn hardcover spines. One shelf is an assortment of bright red bindings, the other a collection in green.

Concentrating on further investigating his bookshelves, pictures in silver frames line one shelf. Narrowing my gaze, I notice a man who—

"That's my family," Nick says behind me, and I jump, as if I was caught snooping. Which I was. "The man with the thick white beard is my father. My mother beside him. My older brother Saint, and my younger sister Kaye."

"You don't talk much about your family."

Nick shrugs. "Not much to say. I'm kind of the black sheep as I didn't stick around to work in the family business."

He mentioned this once before, but he hadn't told me what the business was. And it didn't seem like he was willing to volunteer the information now.

In the picture, Nick and his brother are bundled up in heavy winter coats. His brother looks like him but with a beard that's full of more fluff than black hair. The fur-lined hood over his head gives the brother a modern-day Santa look. Nick is wearing the same bright red cap he wore while putting up lights on my home. His younger sister is dressed in a slim-fitting ski outfit like she's a professional skier or perhaps a model.

"You mentioned you grew up someplace very cold. Where exactly was that?"

"Up North." The vague response has me turning toward him, and he offers me a wineglass. He taps his to mine. "Happy Holiday."

Typically, I hate the sweeping generalization, especially as my name is in the wish. But the way Nick says the phrase, it's as if he's expressing two words, not a single phrase.

Happy. Holliday.

"Merry Christmas," I respond in a voice ripe with anxiety.

Nick lowers to the wooden chair that looks too small for his broad frame. He sips his wine, peering over the rim at me then he sets his glass on the tile flooring before his fireplace.

Taking a sip of wine, I stare back at him before setting my glass on the mantel. A single stocking hangs off-center there.

I'm so out of practice at seducing a man. I want Nick's capable hands on me. I want him to plow my body like he tends my lawn; empty the trash in my head, rid me of my ex; and make me glow like the lights he placed around my house. But I don't know how to start.

Finally, Nick speaks as if reading my thoughts. "Take off your jacket." He pauses, watching me. "Slowly."

With shaky hands, I unbutton the length of my coat. As he demanded, I casually shrug it off my shoulders and let it cascade down my body, eventually pooling at my feet. His Christmas tree is to my back. The flames of his fireplace heat my side, but the light coming from his eyes is set to scorch me.

I'm wearing a bright red dress that wraps over my middle and ties at my hip. I found it in my closet, the tags still on it from a Christmas past when I didn't wear it.

"You're better than sugar plum fairies dancing in my head."

His silly comment lessens some of my anxiety. He tips his head, the movement suggesting I come closer to him. When I stand before him, his hands lift to my hips and coast up my sides, heating my flesh through the thin silk. He pauses just short of my breasts, thumbs scooping underneath them before he slides back down to my hips and lower, tracing the outline of my thighs.

"You make a pretty present." His voice drops as he focuses on the ribbons acting as a belt, securing my dress around my waist. With a lazy tug, he pulls at the tie, stretching it to its full length, which loosens the material. The dress slips open, catching on my breasts. With one finger, Nick reaches forward, swiping the fabric to the left, exposing more of me. The same finger then moves to the right, opening the dress so he has a clear view of my midsection.

"Wanna see how hot my fireplace gets?" A tease fills his voice.

"This is where I should say something witty about logs, right? But I'm too nervous to joke."

His gaze is focused on my face. The intensity in his eyes softens. "We don't have to do anything you don't want to do. Let me look at you, and it will fill my fantasies for another six months."

I tilt my head and my hair shifts over my shoulder. "Fantasies?"

"You're a dream, Holliday. That's why Monica left last summer." His focus remains on me. "I told her I didn't want to continue the casual thing we had going, not when I was having some spectacular dirty thoughts and confusing feelings about my hot neighbor. I couldn't get you out of my head."

His gaze drops, scanning over my body. "I don't need to touch you, honey. But damn, do I want to."

"I want you to touch me." The boldest, truest statement I've ever said.

"Let me unwrap you then."

I nod while I chew on my lower lip.

Nick remains seated. "Take off your dress. Keep the heels on."

Again, I do as he commands, taking my time to brush off one side and then the other, allowing the soft material to skim down my arms and catch on my wrists. I drop my hands, and the dress falls to the floor, circling my feet near my coat.

Vulnerability overcomes me, and I tremble with the need to cover my midsection.

Nick continues to stare at my body, taking his time to gaze from toes to tits. "Come here."

He spreads his thighs, allowing me to step between his legs. Leaning forward, he kisses my belly in several places, taking his time to cover every wrinkle and stretch mark. I've had kids, there's no disguising it on my midsection.

His hands coast up my sides again before cupping my breasts in tandem, pushing them upward and pressing them together. The swells ache, and my nipples strain against the silky fabric of my bra. Cleavage escapes the edges of the material.

Nick runs his nose along the crease between my breasts and then kisses each one. He squeezes until he pinches each nipple.

"Oh, God," I whimper. My lids droop at the sensation rippling over my breasts that haven't been touched by another human in too long.

"Turn around," Nick orders, and I spin. His knees press together and wedge between my legs, forcing me to spread my legs. "Have a seat."

Straddling over his legs, I falter and land on his lap with a thud. "Are you playing Santa again?"

"Let's leave Saint . . . er, Santa out of this. You can tell *me* what you want." He tugs me farther up his thighs. His nose nuzzles at the juncture of my shoulder and neck. "Tell me if you've been bad or good."

Considering I'm a decent person, I definitely haven't ever been as bad as I'd like to be. "You already know I wouldn't mind making the naughty list."

Nick hums at my throat, and his hands stroke my thighs, slipping between them and spreading me wider over his legs. With my back to his chest, my legs bracket his, and I'm feeling very exposed. The scent of my sex mingles with the pine fragrance in the room. I'm wet and wanting, waiting for Nick's next command.

His fingers tickle the insides of my thighs, teasing me as he draws closer to my center. "How naughty do you want to be?"

"Very, please." My own voice is unrecognizable as I sweetly beg.

"Still too polite." He chuckles into my skin while his fingers trail all the way up my legs and stroke over the wetness in my underwear.

I whimper with need.

"You're wet," he murmurs at my ear, kissing just below the lobe. I want his mouth and I turn my head, hoping he'll kiss me like he did during the party. Instead, he presses a kiss to my shoulder while his fingers slip inside my panties. His head pops up, eyes seeking mine. "You're soaked."

He's touched me before. He shouldn't be surprised. Still, I'm embarrassed by how ready I am for him, and I turn away, but he catches my chin and gently forces me to face him. Keeping his eyes on mine, he lazily slips a finger inside my channel.

My breath hitches. My eyes shutter closed. His touch feels incredible as he works his finger in and out. In and out. I'm so wet I hear the suction. He releases my chin, and I twist again, my back fully to his front as he works a second finger into me.

"Look at how I touch you." The command forces my gaze to fall between my thighs, watching him please me inside my underwear. The wooden chair beneath him creaks as my hips start to undulate, working in tandem with his fingers sliding to and fro. I don't know what to do with my hands, so I reach behind me with one arm and cup the back of his head. My other hand rests on my thigh as my leg trembles, and a quake begins. My belly jitters, and my toes curl in my heels.

I can't watch, but I feel . . . *oh, do I feel him.*

"I'm so close," I warn.

"I know, honey. Be naughty on my lap." More words float from his mouth, getting filthier, gaining speed in dirty directions. His thumb presses at my clit, strumming over it.

"Oh God," I whimper again. Like the logs in his fireplace, I crackle and hiss and come apart from the heat racing up my center. The flame is so fast, my breath catches. I sizzle from the release. I want to squeeze my legs together, but he keeps me in place, spread over his thighs as I am, open and exposed. Slowly, I come down from the high, but like a candy cane addict, I want more.

Nick senses my hunger when he frees his fingers but continues to stroke over my sensitive folds. My legs still tremble but my hips rock, eager to keep his attention.

"Gonna get naughtier." He presses me forward to remove me from his lap. I stand with my back to him but glance over my shoulder and watch him unbutton the remaining buttons on his jeans. He shucks them down his hips enough to release a beautiful cock.

Long, and hard, and ready for the taking.

He reaches for a little box on the bookshelf beside him. Inside, he pulls out a foil packet and holds it up for me to see. We don't need to talk about this. He's keeping us both safe, and I dismiss any thoughts of how readily he had a condom available. Once he has himself covered, he reaches for the edge of my underwear and drags it down my legs. For half a second, I can't believe we are really going to do this. For the other half of a second, I'm vibrating with the need to please him. Still glancing over my shoulder, I watch him stroke himself once, twice, before guiding me back over his lap.

"Like this?" Wonder fills my whisper.

"Keeping up the Santa fantasy."

"You said not to mention him," I remind him.

"That I did. But I want you on my lap as you were, begging me to bring out the naughty in you." His voice drops. "Hands on my knees, honey."

I do as he directs, and he lifts me by my hips. He positions himself at my entrance, pausing me in place. "Ready to be a bad girl, Holliday?"

I don't answer before he tugs me downward, allowing my body to draw him in. My nails dig into his kneecaps as my legs spread as wide as they can over his lap. Thank goodness for the heels I'm wearing to stabilize my feet. He drags me down until he's filled me to the hilt.

Sweet peppermint. He holds still, giving my body time to adjust to him.

"Holliday," he murmurs behind me, his voice strained. "I fantasized how it would be with you, but I never . . . not like this . . . it won't be enough."

I don't have time to ask what he means before he's lifting and lowering me, making me ride him like a wild steed. I bounce, and I bump, and I groan as he taps a place inside me that hasn't been tapped in so long.

"Honey," he whispers, picking up the pace as he tugs me down over him and surges up into me. "Touch yourself."

"Oh, God," I purr, sliding my hand between my legs and working my clit as he pistons me over him.

"You're so close," he groans, already reading my body. His encouragement spurs me on.

We might only ever be this one night, but this is what I wanted.

He is my Christmas wish.

"Holliday," he warns, moving me faster, delving deeper, pumping me harder. The rapidness sets off a second spark, and I ignite, coming like I've never come before. I scream, leaning forward as I clutch his kneecaps and cling to his cock inside me.

Nick lifts and lowers me once, twice, a third time and then he stills, growling as he lets go inside me.

"Sweet Holliday," he whispers before lowering his head to my shoulder blade. After a deep exhale, his arms wrap around my waist. He tugs my upper body against his and presses a kiss to my shoulder. "Stay the night."

His request is breathy and desperate, awed even, and my decision comes quickly.

If Santa does exist, he can permanently put me on the naughty list.

The lump of coal in my stocking would be well worth it.

Chapter 9

Shortly after our moment on the chair, Nick moves me, giving me his shirt to cover up. He leads me to the bathroom, where I clean up, and then he brings me a fresh T-shirt to wear. He disappears again but returns to the living room wearing flannel pajama pants and carrying a pile of blankets and pillows. In front of the fireplace, he makes a nest for us on the floor.

Pulling a blanket over my legs, I sit upright while Nick stretches onto his side, and we talk amid the quiet of the crackling fire and the soft glow of his tree.

"May I ask what your family's business is?"

"North Pole Toys." He glances down at the material over my lap.

"*The* North Pole Toys? As in the toy company?" I don't know why I ask. The explanation is in the name. Still, North Pole Toys is a huge company, with delivery service almost anywhere, and a guarantee to find most toys, even high demand ones.

Nick falls to his back. "I try not to make a big deal about it. People assume because I come from money, I have a lot." He rolls his head on the pillow to look up at me. "But I'm not my family. I wanted to work for what I have."

"I get that." Although I'd been taken care of by my parents, I worked in banking for years as a starving post-college student until I met Mitch. He had more wealth than I did.

"When most people learn who my family is, they want favors. Or think I have access to the fortune."

You don't? It's on the tip of my tongue, but I don't ask. That's personal and I don't care about his family's bottom line. I care about him.

"Good thing I'm not most people."

His head shifts. "No, you're quite different than most." A smile fills his voice.

"Nah, I'm just the neighbor." I coyishly wave.

"Don't forget hot. You're the hot neighbor. *My* hot neighbor."

His eyes reflect the flame of the fireplace. Heat builds within them.

"So when you said you know a guy, you meant you really knew someone in the toy industry. That's how you were able to find the Zlot 720 so easily." I'm simply confirming facts. "Shit, I still haven't paid you for it. I promise I will. I don't want you to think I've taken advantage of you."

He gives me a sexy smirk. "You haven't."

Silence floats between us a moment. The atmosphere is even more romantic with us amid the blankets and pillows, and the crackling of the fire.

"Have you thought more about the book you'll write one day?"

I don't miss the positivity in the question. The assurance that I will fulfill that dream someday.

"Oh that." I shrug dismissively. "Not yet."

Nick hums. "What's your favorite holiday tale?"

I stare down at him, cozy and comfortable in our little nest. "*A Christmas Carol* is the only one I can think of." Which is sad considering my college major from a lifetime ago.

"There are so many more good stories than just that classic." He nods toward his colorfully arranged bookshelf.

"I see that." I giggle. "But it's *the* classic, right? The past, present, and future haunt us. But it's also not that simplistic. It's a reminder to be youthful. Not necessarily childlike or childish, because we can never go backward in time. Just be young at heart, I guess. Does that even make sense?"

Nick shifts, perches up on his arm and rests his head on his hand. "Perfect sense."

"It's also a reminder to be present in the present." My brows lift as I give my interpretation and reality slowly sinks in.

Be the light. Nick and I were so playfully reckless when we snuck among the evergreens and then raced through an illuminated garden.

Be present. Nick was also there when I spent the day with my children, forming a new tradition.

He continues to watch me, but a smile crooks the corner of his lips.

"Lastly, it's a message to challenge the future." I pause. "No, change it. Be the future you want to be."

Nick sits upright, leaning on his arm for support. "Sounds like you might be onto something. A great lesson for children. Or even adults."

While he stares at me, I glance down at the blankets over my lap, considering all I'd just said. He has no idea how close he is to the truth of what I want to write.

"It's *your* future, Holliday. Do what makes you happiest."

I lift my head. "Is that what you did by becoming a fireman?"

"Exactly. The family business was never going to be mine. It was always my older brother's destiny. And while I could have been in marketing, or research and development, I chose me instead. I wanted to *do* something, not make something." He watches me as he continues, "Right now, you're doing something. You're a bank teller, but it's passive, not passionate, when you've been called to be creative, and make something. Neither path is right or wrong, just different for each of us."

I sigh and slowly nod. I hear him. I believe in what he's saying, I just don't know how to apply it. I'm not ready to write a children's book. Maybe, someday, but right now I have children to raise, a mortgage to pay, and that means I need a steady paycheck from the bank.

"Reading all these books is how you got so smart?" I tease, tilting my head toward the bookshelves.

"I'm more than a pretty face," he jokes, the twinkle in his eye flickering.

Laughter fills my throat. "You're cocky."

"Hmm. I'll show you cocky." His arm wraps around my waist and he takes me down to the pillows behind me. Then he kisses me, slow and sweet. He tastes like peppermint, smells like snow, and the room around us is fragrant with balsam. The heady combination draws me under his spell and soon he's over me, between my thighs.

"I want you again," he whispers between kisses.

"I'm all yours."

And he isn't *so* cocky as he takes his time to discover me and allow me to explore him. The intimacy feels like we're making love, not just having neighborly sex. Tears prickle my eyes with the care and homage he pays my body. I warn myself not to let emotion get in the way. *Falling* in love is not on my Christmas DO list.

Instead, I feel. My skin is electric. My heart at full wattage. From Nick's sensual attention, I glow like the star on the top of his tree.

+ + +

At the sharp sound of car doors slamming shut, I bolt upright.

"What time is it?" The question is groggy and sleep-filled despite my lack of sleep last night.

Nick and I talked for hours after round two, and then we passed out before the lingering warmth of his turned off fireplace. (Fire safety, of course).

Nick shifts. I'd been tucked into his chest, his arm over my waist, and his heat keeping me peacefully toasty.

When another car door slams, I spring from the floor and rush to the front window.

"Shit," I mutter.

"What's wrong?" Nick grumbles, exhausted. He had the party on Friday night and worked all day Saturday, then spent most of last night awake.

"Mitch brought the kids home early."

"What time is it?" Nick sits up, scratching underneath his chin. The scruff along his throat appears to have thickened overnight. Hair sticks up on one side of his head. He's adorably sleepy and I want to crawl back into our little cocoon of blankets, but I can't.

I need to figure out how to get over there from here without my ex or my kids catching me.

"Early." *Damn Mitch.* He's done it again, bringing the kids home before his time ends. "I don't know what to do."

Nick shifts, lifting his legs and spreading his bent knees to balance his arms over them. "Act like you came over to borrow sugar."

"What?" *In a red dress meant for seduction?*

"Put your shoes and your coat on. Button up. I'll get some sugar. Pretend like it just happened." His eyes harden a bit at the lie I need to act out, but I don't have a choice. My kids are heading for my house, and I'm not home when my SUV is clearly in the driveway.

I rush for my heels, slipping into them with a groan. I don't wear such high shoes anymore. Reaching for my coat, I shrug it on and button it up. Mitch won't know the walk of shame I've got going on underneath which is a man's T-shirt and my underwear.

While I hustle to dress, Nick slowly rises and enters his kitchen, returning with a small package of sugar. "Take the whole thing."

"You're an angel," I groan, hastily turning for the door, but Nick catches my arm and I spin to face him. His hands cup my jaw. The kiss is sizzling hot, and I wish I could stay longer.

"I've got to go," I mumble against his tempting mouth.

"But I want you to stay." He chuckles as he releases me and then follows me to the door.

When I step out, I expect Nick to shut the door behind me, but he doesn't. He steps onto his front stoop, bare foot and bare chested despite the sharp December temperature.

"Mommy," Nash calls out, sweet and excited as he sees me crossing Nick's small yard for our shared driveway.

"Hey baby. Just getting some sugar from the neighbor." I lift the bag as proof of my mission, fighting the heat that rushes up my neck and flames my cheeks.

Mitch narrows his eyes, watching me wobble in my heels. I'm walking through the thin layer of freshly fallen snow.

My ex might have been an attractive man at one point, but all his good looks vanished the moment he cheated on me. Standing in jeans and a puffy winter coat, with a questioning expression on his clean-shaven face, he's just a man.

"What do we need sugar for?" Eloise asks, as all three of them wait for me on my front stoop.

"Cookies." My answer is a little too enthusiastic and not at all what I'd planned to do today. But suddenly, Christmas cookies are on the agenda.

"Is Nick going to make cookies with us?" Nash asks, excited by the prospect.

"Oh. Uh, I'm sure he has other things to do today." I glance over my shoulder to see my neighbor still standing on his stoop, leaning casually against the railing, watching me.

"Mitch, you remember Nick, right?" I brusquely point in Nick's direction.

"Yeah, no." His squinty glare turns toward the man next door.

"Well, he lent me some sugar." I hold the bag up again as if Mitch hadn't already seen it. "You're back early." I bite back the venom I want to spew at my ex for his blatant disregard for our schedule. I'm not upset to see my kids early, but it's upsetting that their father doesn't spend his maximum time with them.

"Paige wasn't feeling well."

"Christmas is too exciting for her," Eloise mumbles, sarcasm lacing her eight-year-old voice, proof she doesn't believe whatever that statement is meant to mean.

I don't care one fig for Paige or her Christmas excitement, or lack thereof. "Okay, well. The kids are home now, so . . ." *Piss off*, I want to say but I bite my tongue.

"See you Christmas morning," Mitch says, as if confirming with me what's been set in stone since our signatures dried on the divorce papers.

"The kids have their Christmas musical on Thursday night," I remind him, which is something he's needed reminding of three times now in the same number of weeks.

"Right." He nods once, signifying he isn't going to remember, which means he might not show up. However, I won't confront him in front of the kids. I just want him gone and I sneak a peek in the direction of the house next door where the owner has returned to the warmth of his home.

A cold gust of air rushes up my coat and I shiver.

"You're kind of overdressed for a bag of sugar," Mitch comments.

"Grabbed the closest pair of shoes and my long coat." I brush past him because he doesn't deserve an explanation and open my front door. "Okay, guys. Say bye to Dad."

"Bye, Dad," they say in unison and then each take a turn hugging him.

"Christmas morning," Mitch confirms once more, eyeing me as I stand in my entryway, door open but not inviting him in. He takes in the high heels I haven't worn in years. My bare legs are pebbled from the cold. And my long coat hits my kneecaps and hints I'm not wearing much else beneath it. Once upon a time, he'd give me a look after pleasantly inspecting me and I'd easily fall for it.

Never again, buddy.

"Christmas morning," I confirm, my tone sharp. "Bye, Mitch."

Once I close the door, I fall against the barrier and let out an exasperated chuckle. My phone pings in my pocket.

What time should I be over to make cookies?

I bite my lip, fight the giddy bubbles in my throat, but I can't help the smile warming my cheeks.

Seems Santa has a helper and he's willing to bake with me.

+ + +

Nick arrives an hour later with a to-go mug of coffee for him, and hot chocolate for me. Plus, another handful of greenery.

"Is that a sprig of holly?" The uniquely shaped leaf is the quintessential Christmas decoration, complete with a few red berries.

"Yes, it is." He smiles before handing over the cluster. He's so sweet and original.

When we enter my kitchen, he claps his hands and addresses the kids coloring at the table. "What kind of cookies are we making?"

"I don't even know if I have all the ingredients for any recipe." I dig my fingers into my freshly washed hair and hold it behind my neck.

"What do you typically make?"

Despite the question, I take a moment to appreciate this man standing in my kitchen, acting as if baking Christmas cookies isn't something special, when it's a once-a-year occasion.

"Peanut butter blossoms. Russian tea cakes. Sometimes holly wreaths. The ones with corn flakes and red-hot candies." I definitely don't have corn flakes or red hots.

"Don't forget peppermint ones," Nash says from his place at the kitchen table. He said he didn't eat breakfast so a bowl of dry cereal rests beside his coloring sheet.

"What are peppermint ones?"

"Oh. I kind of invented those myself. It's just sugar cookies with peppermint sticks crushed up and added into the mix. Plus, a splash of peppermint extract."

Nick's brows lift. "Sounds amazing."

"They're *sooooo* good," Nash agrees, speaking while chewing.

"And sugar cookies," Eloise adds. "Do we still have the cut-outs?" She's been quiet since returning from her father's place and I haven't had a minute to address if something happened while she was gone.

Why would we not have the cookie cutters? Mitch got the house in our divorce. I got the holiday cookie cutters. I hold my sarcasm and answer her. "Of course, I still have them."

A weak smile forms on her little mouth. My brows pinch and I glance at Nick who has been watching her as well. His questioning eyes meet mine, but I don't have an explanation.

"Okay. Who's ready for cookie making?" Nick starts opening my cabinets, hunting for ingredients without an official recipe in hand.

"I might need to go to the store." I'm certain I don't have half the things we'll need.

"No worries," Nick says, rummaging through my cupboard. "Whatever you don't have, I might have at my place."

I stare at him, shifting around spices and pulling out vanilla extract, like he's completely comfortable in my home. Like he belongs here.

He turns to give me a smile, and his signature wink. "I already gave you my sugar."

I roll my lips and fight a giggle. He gave me sugar alright.

"Okay. Cookie time," I call out and both my kids cheer, returning Eloise to her energetic self.

+ + +

Hours later, my countertops and dining room table are covered in an array of cookies. Nick had all the ingredients I didn't, and we baked more cookies than my family of three could ever eat.

"I think I'll make up little tins and have the kids give most of these to the neighbors."

My children lost their interest in baking a while ago and went off to play with the wooden train set underneath our tree. Another new tradition established this year.

"That's the spirit." Nick's bright expression shows his pleasure at my suggestion.

"It's only cookies," I brush off.

"It's generosity."

I pause. Does he think I'm *not* generous? I mean, he gave me four orgasms where I only gave him two last night but I'm hoping he doesn't consider me too greedy in that area.

Still, I can admit that Nick has done more for me than I've done for him this holiday season.

Donate time.

He's given me an invaluable gift but what have I done for him?

"What happened to your list?" Nick says, staring at my fridge and the magnetic clip still at an angle from when I tugged the list free.

"Oh, I . . . I lost it." I chew my lip, attempting to wrestle back the lie.

As if Nick knows I'm not telling the truth he turns toward me, watching me. "Huh."

"It was only a list." I shrug. "I make plenty of them." Full of things I'll never complete or achieve.

"Remember, I know when you're lying," he says, lowering his voice and tapping the side of his temple.

"Well, considering the whole bad and good thing, we've already established I'm a little bad." Still a good person, but not without my faults.

Nick gives me his full attention, adding that flirty eye twitch while whispering, "Very bad."

"Speaking of bad . . ." I cross the kitchen for my living room and lift a gift I've placed beneath my tree. My children have moved from playing with the train to watching a holiday movie. "I have a present for you."

"You didn't have to do that." His smile hints he's pleased, though. Who doesn't like to receive gifts, like he once said to me.

"It isn't as great as what you gave me," I whisper, holding his gaze at the reminder of the robe, negligee, and adult-only toy.

"Did you go out purposely seeking this gift for me?" His question suggests intention. I wanted to give him something. He nods at the package I still hold. "Were you excited to purchase it for me?"

"Well, when I saw it, I thought of you." The item spoke to me.

His gaze lifts to meet my eyes. "You think of me?"

Of course, I think of him. Probably a little too much lately. Chewing on my lower lip, I fight a grin.

When I don't answer, he reaches forward, making grabby fingers. "Okay, well, give it to me."

Smiles light up both our faces. "You can open it now. It's seasonally appropriate."

Nick enthusiastically rips the carefully wrapped package, with childlike eagerness on full display. When he opens the box, he's careful as he pulls out the heavy snow globe.

"The evergreen forest reminded me of the night we went to the Botanic Gardens. The snow-couple are dancing." Also reminding me of that night. "And I thought since I dressed like a snowwoman for the fundraiser, maybe you'd be reminded of me when you look at them."

As Nick continues to stare at the item, I'm rethinking my explanation, feeling like it's rom-com nonsense. He flips the globe to make it snow and the flakes float downward, over the trees, like the lights that danced over us when we were among them.

"And . . ." I reach for the snow globe and wind the key on the underside. My voice lowers, concerned that he'll think the gift is hokey. "It plays our song."

A tinny rendition of "Christmas Time Is Here" plays.

After a round of music, Nick slowly looks up at me. "You're unforgettable, Holliday. Thank you. This means a lot to me."

His Adam's apple bobs and his cheeks turn rosy. If I didn't know better, I'd say he almost looks choked up by the gift, but that can't be true. No, his expression is the same as that day last summer when I asked him if he was okay. Before he cut my grass and we knew one another. He looks stunned. Surprised maybe, but also a little sad.

Nick steps toward me, softly kissing my cheek. With the kids in the room, it's more than I would have expected.

"I'll put it on my mantel where I can see it, and think of you, more than I already do every day."

"You think of me?" I tease to lighten the moment, but I already feel light, almost giddy, that my gift is having such an effect on him.

"Probably more than I should," he says as if reading my thoughts. "Thank you."

When he pulls me in for an additional hug, the embrace is more than gratitude. His firm arms hold tight, keeping me against him. His free hand cups the back of my head. He breathes in at my neck. This is a hug.

Give hugs.

And I can't remember the last time someone hugged me. Not my children. Not my parents. But a genuine hold-on-to-me squeeze from someone I care about and who might care about me, too.

BE THE FUTURE YOU WANT

Chapter 10

With a house fragrant from baking and a warmth in my belly from another wonderful day being present with my children, Eloise and Nash settle into Nash's bed, and I read them one of the many versions we own of *'Twas The Night Before Christmas.* This is another classic tale, although officially a poem, about a man and the night Santa arrives. What he sees. What he hears. And the cheer brought to him by the experience.

Once I finish reading, I snuggle Nash, peppering kisses over his face and giving him one more hug before turning on his nightlight and leading Eloise to her room.

She climbs into her bed, slips underneath the blankets and sighs.

"That's a heavy sound." I tuck the blankets tighter around her chest as she crosses her arms above the comforter.

"Can Santa really get into our house without a chimney?"

I sigh next. "You remember we watched that movie where a fireplace magically appeared in an apartment that didn't have one, and Santa came down the chimney to leave presents." I tug the blankets tighter and lean down to rub my nose along hers. "Don't you worry, Santa will find a way to visit us."

"Will he break in?"

"Heaven's no. Why would you say that?"

"When Paige was having too much Christmas excitement, she said Santa will just break into our house to leave presents if we don't have a chimney."

What the hell? Suddenly, Christmas excitement sounds like code for too much alcohol, and perhaps Miss Paige was hungover this morning which is why Mitch returned the kids early. But still, what is she thinking to tell a child someone will break into our house like a criminal to leave gifts? I'd call Mitch out on this, but I prefer to reserve my energy for being present and the light for my children. Besides, calling him out would be a waste of time.

"Maybe we should go home for Christmas."

"Home?" I blink.

"To our house. Where Paige and Daddy live. We had a fireplace there. We can't even hang stockings here."

The stockings. They're draped over the back of a chair waiting for me to figure out how and where to hang them.

Taking a deep breath, my head hangs. "Baby, *this* is our home now. Our house for the three of us, Nash, you, and me." I sternly add, "And Santa will not break into our house. He's resourceful, not a deviant."

"What's resourceful mean?" Her innocent little eyes look up at me.

"It means, he'll find a safe, secure way to bring you presents, my good girl." I tap her nose.

"What's deviant mean?"

Your father and his new girlfriend. "A bad person. And we both know Santa is a good man."

Eloise watches me, questions still in her eyes. I'm not ready for her to stop believing in the man in red or thinking the world is full of deviants, either breaking into homes or wrecking them with adultery.

"Santa is going to love the cookies you made for him today."

"His belly is going to be so full after he goes from house to house to house." A twinkle returns to her eyes. "I hope Elfie doesn't steal any cookies tonight."

Oh boy, now I'll have to pretend the elf nibbled a cookie and left a little mess of crumbs despite his theft. Breaking in Santas. Cookie stealing elves. What's next on the list? Bad-boy next-door neighbors?

"I'll seal them all up tight. And tomorrow night we can deliver some to the neighbors."

"Can we sing at their front doors, like Carol does?"

I laugh. "You mean, carolers. And I'll think about it." I'm not known for my ability to carry a tune.

"I need to practice for the musical on Thursday." Her expression shifts to concentration and a sprinkle of too-serious for an eight-year-old.

"You're going to be great. Now, time to sleep, so sugar plum fairies can dance in your head."

She lifts her arms and I lean down, wrapping her in another hug, holding on a little longer myself because I don't want her to grow up yet.

+ + +

In the darkness of my house, I sit before my Christmas tree staring at the low lights, thinking about the past year. Mitch and Paige. What Paige said. Eloise and Nash and the changes we've had to make this year. Home.

This house is our home now, and as time has passed, I find I don't miss the too-large space in the suburbs. Our city home has character and charm, even if the closets are a bit small. Our street is friendly without being nosy, and my next-door neighbor is wonderful.

I don't question if Nick and I will have a repeat of what we did. For now, I revel in gratitude for making love with him.

And having my children snug in their beds.

And a roof over our heads with a house I pay for from the paycheck I earn for the work that I do.

Nick's words come back to me, though. Doing something or making something are both vocations. Being physical or creative are both strengths. And I wasn't certain I was using all of mine.

My phone buzzes beside me on the couch and I lift it to read the message.

You left your tree on.

Nosy little neighbor next door. **I'm still up.**

Nick left earlier, with another fireman 'thing' as his reason. He was playing Santa at a children's hospital.

Suddenly, my phone rings.

"Hey."

"Hey," he replies, his voice warm like cinnamon. "Why are you still awake?"

"You're the one who must be exhausted." After a vigorous night, followed by a long day spent making Christmas cookies on his day off.

"Yeah, but I can sleep tomorrow." He works two days on, two days off. "So, answer my question. What's on your mind?"

"Eloise is having doubts about Santa again. I don't think I'm doing a good job this year, and I'm worried this might be the last year she believes."

Nick chuckles. "I'm in my forties and *I* still believe in him."

I weakly smile although he can't see me.

"But Christmas isn't really about a man in a red suit with a jolly smile and a white beard. It's a feeling, honey. It's magic and mystery. And it's belief in the good in people."

"I know, but I'm struggling to explain that to my eight-year-old."

"That's because children need something concrete until they can understand the abstract. A man passing out presents as a reward for good behavior might seem archaic but it's also a phase until children can be the present. Give rather than receive."

I nod. "Eloise said she wanted to go home tonight. Our former house had a fireplace." My eyes suddenly prickle with tears over something so silly as a fireplace and a previous life. "I'm worried I'm not building a home here."

"Honey, *you* are their home. Comfort and joy. Safety and peace. Look at today. It doesn't matter where you made those cookies, it's the time you spent together. Same with chopping down a tree and starting a new tradition. She'll see that your house gives her something equally magical as the old place. Maybe even more special than years past."

"Yeah, maybe."

"Holliday." He sighs, compassion in the breathy exhale. "You have a great house, but you and your kids make it a home."

He was right. It didn't matter if we lived here or there, my children were what made any house feel like our home.

"I should let you go. I need to work tomorrow and you need sleep."

A weighty silence falls between us, and I wish Nick could come over, hug me like he did earlier, and stay the night, just holding me tight, offering comfort and quiet joy.

"Peace, Holliday. Sleep well. Nestle into your kerchief. I'll be putting on my nightcap."

A strong laugh bursts forth. I'd like to see him in his red cap with nothing else on his glorious body.

"Night, Nick."

Send Peace.

He's been an olive branch.

+ + +

The next four days go by in a flurry of activity. Final dance lessons for Eloise. Final karate class for Nash. The last week of school before a break, which leads to overexcitement and high energy with emotional breakdowns or sugar crashes, depending on the day. And of course, a last-minute costume needed for the Christmas musical.

How the heck was I supposed to find green sweatpants the night before the show during freakin' Christmas?

When Thursday night arrives, Mitch does not show for our kids' holiday performance. His excuse involved drinks with a customer. More *Christmas excitement* for him and Paige.

I had considered asking Nick if he'd like to attend, but it seemed like a big ask. We haven't crossed paths in days, not since the glorious night we spent together, or the day we shared with my children baking cookies. While I worked, he undoubtedly slept. Then he had two twelve-hour shifts. He'd sent a simple text to say he hoped to see me soon. Still, the relative silence between us has been unnerving.

My parents attended the concert, applauding loudly and taking a million pictures before inviting the kids and I out for ice cream afterwards.

And, by Friday morning I'm on edge.

No apology from Mitch about his no-show.

No text from Nick.

By the time I'm taking my lunch break in the staff lounge, I'm irritable about the most minute things, like my lackluster lunch of a peanut butter sandwich and apple slices. Randomly, I scroll through emails, swiping past promotions for shoes I can't afford and vacation suggestions I desperately want to take when I pause at an email from the bank.

Clicking on the email, it opens, and I scan the notice.

I read it twice. Blink. And read it one more time.

Tears should be clouding my vision, but I'm too stunned to react. Or maybe I'm too angered to respond.

My hands begin to shake, though. My breath holds for a second as disbelief and bewilderment kick in next. Then an ache presses at my sternum, and squeezes my ribs, suppressing my airways.

This cannot be happening.

Hastily, I exit the lunchroom, leaving my unfinished sandwich behind and cross the bank lobby to the manager's office. My low heels clack against the tile floor, matching the heavy rhythm of my heart, until I reach my boss's office.

"Is this a joke?" I ask, holding up my phone, face out for Dominique to see.

"I'm afraid not." Seated behind her desk, Dominique lowers her eyes.

"What does it mean?" I ask as if I hadn't read the simple words three times.

"Just what it says," she lowers her voice. "The bank is downsizing, and—"

"You couldn't have warned me?"

She rolls her lips inward. What a fucking coward. She had to have known this was going to happen.

"It's Christmas." My throat clogs and I choke on the sob that hasn't quite decided if it wants to be disbelieving laughter or a sudden burst of tears.

"I'm sorry." There's no sympathy in my boss's apology. "You're free to leave early. And you'll be paid for the next two weeks."

I've taken my remaining vacation days for the year to accommodate the kids' school break. I have the next two weeks off.

This is bullshit, I want to scream but I'm trying to remain professional despite the fact the bank management clearly is not.

Because at noon on a Friday, days before Christmas, I've been told by email, that I'm being let go.

Chapter 11

I don't remain in the bank. I don't say goodbye to my colleagues. I don't explain myself to Dominique. I leave and drive straight home.

There I kick off my heels and peel myself out of my work slacks. I nearly rip the buttons from my blouse while removing it as if the clothing is burning me alive.

I can't believe this.

Within minutes, my phone rings, but I ignore it. I'll need to call my parents and tell Mitch, although explaining what happened to all of them will feel like another failure. I've done nothing wrong, other than be the last person hired in the hierarchy of seniority where the bank decided to make financial cuts, including downsizing staff, before a new year rings in.

Slipping into comfy leggings and an oversize sweatshirt, I ignore my phone as it rings again. I'm not ready to talk to anyone, and I can't imagine someone from the bank calling me to either apologize, admit they made a mistake, or ask me to come back.

I'm simply a cog in their business wheel. One they no longer need although I need to pay a mortgage and feed my kids. Mitch has been late on child support again. And he never offered to pay half of the overly expensive Christmas presents *he* promised our children Santa would deliver.

As I slowly descend my stairs, a sharp hammering on my front door rattles the thing. Through the transom window, I see a familiar red cap.

Is he kidding me? Now, he wants to see me.

Still, I reach for the knob and hastily open the door. Our eyes lock.

"You're home early." The corner of his mouth curls in that sexy manner that might have me begging him to tear off my panties if my mind wasn't other places.

"What do you want, Nick?" I snap.

"What's wrong?" His flirtatious smirk slides away as he stiffens, straightening to his full height.

Swiping my hand through my hair, I cup the back of my neck and tip my head backward. "The bank let me go."

Instantly, he's in my house and I'm in his arms, and he's clutching me to his chest like he's just saved me from a fire.

"I'm so sorry, honey," he mutters against my hair, holding me like he won't let go and I can only fantasize that he won't. Because it's been four flippin' days of white-out from him.

My door is kicked shut without him releasing me, and then he's moving us further into my house and away from the cold entryway.

"What happened?" he asks once we stand in my living room.

"Cutbacks." I sigh. "Newest hire goes first." I point at myself before breaking away from him and rounding for the couch, collapsing onto the cushions.

Nick follows, sitting beside me, and slips his arm around my shoulders, tugging me to his chest. His lips meet my hair and linger there. "I'm so sorry."

After a long silence, Nick mutters, "What can I do?"

Hold me. Never let me go. "Is it too early to drink copious amounts of wine?" I'm kidding. Kind of.

"Where are the kids?"

I pull back and stare at him. "School. Their break starts later today." I have three hours, but I can't show up shitfaced to pick them up.

"Okay. One glass. On it." Nick jumps up, like he's happy he has something to do rather than sit beside a sad, pathetic loser who lost her first job after years out of the job market.

I'll just start over. Again.

A new year, a new job. Again.

A bulbous glass of wine appears before me, filled almost to the rim with peppery red. "You can chug it or pace yourself, but you're only getting the one glass before we pick up your kids."

Nick falls back to the couch with a hefty thud, and I take a hardy guzzle of wine while his hand smooths up my back.

I have no idea what I'll do next, but I can't think about that right now. Almost one year from learning about Mitch's infidelity, and I feel no further ahead in my life.

How will I afford my home?

How will I cover my bills?

How will I feed my kids?

Glancing forward, that righteous elf sits on the china cabinet glaring down at me. Judging me.

"Hey," Nick purrs beside me. "Don't overthink things yet. One day at a time, and at this point, one hour at a time."

I nod before tipping up my glass and taking another deep gulp. My hand trembles, and the tears hit. I cover my face with my palm, tucking my head forward and allowing my hair to curtain me from Nick watching me unravel.

"Hey," he murmurs again, taking the glass from me and setting it on the low table before us. Next, his arms wrap around me, and I'm tugged down to the couch, snuggled into his chest, and inhaling his bayberry and snow scent as tears soak his shirt. I cry for what's lost. I cry for the unknown. I might even cry a little in relief as I didn't love my job.

Still, the tears fall, and I breathe in Nick. The comfort of him. The strength of his arms around me. The sense that it will be okay. Maybe not today. Maybe not tomorrow, but I'll figure this out . . . like I always do.

Time passes. I'm not certain how long, but I drift into a cozy sleep as my body shuts down from stress.

When a phone pings, I sit upright, pressing into Nick's firm chest to notice his phone face up on the table.

"What is that?" I ask, my voice hoarse as his phone lights up with a background image that's familiar to me.

"Oh, it's nothing." He taps the home button to brush away the screen saver, but it's too late.

With my legs tangled in his, and a sleepy look on his face, I stare down at him.

"Was that my list?" The DO list I'd written out and hung on my fridge but eventually threw away. He'd taken a picture of it, but he'd also added his own graphics. Squiggly lines from the pencil feature in photo edits on his phone mark up the list. As if he's been checking off the things he's done . . . for me.

Be the light. Check.

Be present. Check.

Donate food. Modified to time and check.

Wrap someone in a hug. Check.

Send Peace. Check.

The only one not marked off is *Make Love*, because clearly the night last weekend meant more to me than my player neighbor.

The blow comes on top of the pressure of losing my job. All those soft words and sweet moments meant nothing to him while my feelings are real and deep. He's been a beacon of light during my dark holiday stupor and just when I was starting to feel sexy, confident, and free, this happens.

"Am I some kind of charity case to you?" I press harder at his chest, wrestling to untangle my legs from his and scramble to the opposite end of the couch. Nick swings his legs to sit upright and face me.

I swipe both my hands into my hair, feeling dirty and cheap. My skin now crawls with the idea that this man did all these *things* with me. Disappointment strikes like a snowball to the chest.

"No," he huffs, like I'm joking with him, when the joke is on me.

"Then what is that?" I wave at his phone, staring at the now blank screen. "Am I some kind of seasonal project to you? You're Santa's helper, assisting the pathetic single mom next door."

"Holliday," he groans. "It's not like that. Not at all."

Pressing into the cushion, I rush upward, catching myself as my balance wavers. The one glass of wine went to my head, and the little nap didn't help.

"But isn't it?" My voice rises, and I tug at my hair. "You've cut my grass. Shoveled my drive. Hung my lights." Dropping my hands, I wave around me. "And I'm so appreciative, but you . . . you only feel sorry for me, don't you?"

"How can you say that? I don't pity you. How the hell can I pity you when you're the strongest, most capable, brilliant, and caring woman I've ever met?" He sighs heavily. "The thing is, you don't have to do it all alone all the time."

Nick's words are so at odds with his actions; both a balm and a splinter to my heart. I can't believe he sees me that way. Strong. Capable. Brilliant? Yet for days, he's been relatively silent.

"What I don't need is you, Nick." The words are the sharp saw against a tree trunk, grating and rough, slicing at the base before the loud thunk of it falling over.

"Wow," Nick says, pushing to his feet to face me.

We stare at each other.

"You know what? Maybe you should stop writing lists and start writing your future."

I gasp, straightening as tall as I can. What a low blow on this day of all days. "I think you should go."

His hands come to his hips, and he turns his head as if I've slapped him. His verbal assault on me feels like a sucker punch to the gut.

And I don't need this right now. I don't need him, and I don't want to be his little project anymore.

Finally, he turns back to me, glaring at me with those intensely blue eyes, now almost dark as coal. I cross my arms to protect myself, or maybe to hold myself together. He needs to go, even if deep down I really want him to stay.

He swipes up his phone and rounds the couch, stopping just short of my front hall. "How will Eloise and Nash get home today?"

I close my eyes at the stab to my chest. At the painful thought that he's still being considerate and thinking of them.

"I'll call my mother." Maybe my parents can take the kids for the night, so I can re-evaluate my life and the shitshow it still is.

While I remain by the couch, Nick reaches for my front door. The sound of it opening has me holding my breath. Then he steps back into view and stares at me.

"Did you ever think that this was never about *you* needing *me*?"

My mouth pops open, but Nick disappears from view again, the door to my home softly clicking closed at his exit.

Never about me?

All those odd jobs Nick did. All the time spent with me and my kids. Did he need us? Was this never about me needing help, being pitied or a charity case, but simply, possibly, that *he* wanted to feel needed. He wanted to be near us. Near me.

The confusing thoughts mingle with my already frayed nerves, and I collapse to the couch once again, crying like I haven't cried in a year.

Somehow, this heartbreak feels so much worse.

My DO list is done.

+ + +

It's late when I hear the sharp slam of a truck door in the driveway. Laying flat on my back in my bed, I stare up at the ceiling.

My parents took the kids for the night as I told them I had some last-minute shopping to do, and I wanted to wrap presents without the kids home.

I'll tell them the truth tomorrow.

Day One again.

Rolling on my side, I stare at my window, where I wouldn't be able to see Nick's house anyway. Still, he's over there.

Is he alone? Is it my business?

I didn't need him, as I'd abruptly declared earlier.

But I wanted him.

What Nick offered was more than mowing my lawn, hanging up lights, and snuggling before a fireplace. His gift had been him. His friendship. His presence. He'd been in his best form, doing things for me, but he also sensed what I needed.

Support. Kindness. Love.

What had I done for him?

I recall asking him last summer if he was okay, sensing a kindred spirit in his stoic sadness. Thinking back, I recall his reaction, then compared that to his reaction to my snow globe gift.

Perhaps, no one's thought of Nick's feelings in a while. Maybe no one's given him such a thoughtful gift, one full of memory and meaning. It could be that something's lacking in his life, which is what called me to him in the first place.

And for all the things he'd done for me, hadn't I done something in return? He mowed my lawn. I bought him a plant. He trimmed bushes. I'd made him a casserole. He played catch with Nash or let Eloise make chalk drawings in his driveway. I'd give him cookies.

We'd been doing this dance for months.

For some reason, Dr. Suess came to mind. That saying about Christmas not coming from a store. Maybe Christmas meant a little bit more.

Nick was that more.

And just maybe . . . I'd been more to him as well.

Chapter 12

Over the weekend, I hear Nick tinkering in his yard. The buzz of a saw. The whirl of a drill. The sharp clap of a power hammer. It's like the Universe wants to remind me he's right next door. But despite my deeper feelings toward Nick, I'm still angry and confused.

By Monday, the first official day of my kids' winter break, and my first day of unemployment, I'm irritated. Or maybe I'm just overwhelmed. My mind is pulled in a million different directions.

Eloise and Nash deserve this time off from school, but I'm already concerned about when the new year starts, and I don't have a job.

I'm broken again, feeling a bit defeated, and mustering enthusiasm for the holidays is exhausting. Pretending I'm okay for my kids zaps my energy.

However, sitting in the house and wallowing isn't an option. Instead, I declare we need a field trip to celebrate their first day off.

Like a hundred other families, we go to Maggie Daley Park Ice Skating Rink. The crisp, cold outdoors does wonders for my mind as I'm too busy concentrating on helping Nash to worry about my future. Eloise effortlessly weaves through the people wobbling on two thin blades, while I glide alongside Nash, holding his hand as he swishes back and forth on shaky legs.

"You're doing great, buddy." His little legs *swish-swish* while his tongue pops out, rolling around his mouth like it helps him keep his balance.

As we round a bend, in the distance, a fire engine siren rips through the air, cutting into the festive holiday music played on overhead speakers throughout the park.

"Did you know Nick is a fireman?" Nash says to me.

"I did know that." Nash often mentions this fact when he sees or hears a fire truck.

"I really had fun with him when we went to chop down our Christmas tree. And when he made cookies with us."

"Oh, yeah?" I stare forward as Nash's blades *scrape-scrape* over the bumpy ice.

"Dad doesn't do those kinds of things."

My chest aches. Mitch didn't do much regarding the holidays. I'd done it all, so I don't know why I felt this year would be so different. I was still making lists, checking them twice, and doing all the holiday things.

Baking. Buying. Wrapping. Decorating.

It was the same old, same old. Only, it wasn't. We'd made new traditions this year. The three of us.

However, Nick was sprinkled into most of those newly made memories. He'd played a big part in attempts to restore my faith in this season.

"Think Nick would like to go ice skating with us?" Nash asks. His arms wave awkwardly at his sides, like a winterized Frankenstein learning to skate.

"I don't know, Nash. He's busy."

Nash scrunches up his face as he teeters, and I catch him by the back of his coat. He straightens and continues.

"He said he'd never be too busy for us. Not like Dad. Dad is always busy."

"He what?" I'm the one to falter, my skates catching on a notch of ice along the path.

"Dad's always saying he's busy."

I'd heard that excuse plenty of times before but that isn't what I'm asking. "I mean, Nick. When did he say he was never too busy for us." I correct myself. "For you."

Nash shrugs, causing his body to wobble again. "When we went to cut down our tree. He said if I ever needed anything I could ask him. If I was in trouble, or you needed help, I could come to his house."

My brows pinch. "What did he mean by trouble?" Just what was he suggesting to my son?

"He said if something happened to our house, or I didn't feel safe. I should never hide in a fire, but if someone breaks in, then I should hide. He also told me to call 9-1-1, but I told him I don't have a cell phone."

Oh my God, what was Nick thinking by saying such things to my child? I already had Eloise afraid Santa was a burglar.

"Why did Nick say all that?"

"He said he just wanted me to know he'd always be there to protect us."

I still as Nash skates ahead, his stance a little more confident. His strides better. *I'd* always be here to protect him and Eloise, but it was nice to think someone else might be looking out for them as well.

Looking out for all of us.

And like a freaking sign from the Universe, "Christmas Time Is Here" begins to play over the loudspeaker.

+ + +

After ice skating, the kids and I go to Ashford's to look at the famous department store's holiday window display. Each year the windows along State Street are decorated according to a theme, often related to something whimsical and seasonal. One year was centered around Dr. Seuss. Another was *The Nutcracker*. This year's storyline revolves around a toy soldier, and his desire to be home for the holidays.

Nash is mesmerized by the intricate movements of the puppet characters. Eloise enjoys the display, too, but it's lacking the glitter and glitz she requires to make something Christmas-y.

The common word 'holiday' blends in around us and I've learned to distinguish a call for me from the mundane mention. So, it isn't until someone catches my arm that I jerk and turn to face Eva, from the Snowball's Chance party.

"I thought that was you," she says. Her eyes are bright. Her cheeks rosy from the cold. "I've been meaning to call you."

My brows lift, surprised. I'd forgotten we'd exchanged phone numbers the night of the fundraiser.

"Since the winter break is finally here, I thought we could maybe get together with the kids. Have a playdate."

I glance down at the little girl around Eloise's age who holds Eva's hand. A riot of blonde curls cascade beneath a pink knit hat with a pom on the top.

"This is Tam."

"Hi, Tam." I wave. "This is Eloise." I slip my arm around my girl. "And Nash." His focus is still on a soldier marching in place while the mechanics of the display make the puppet look like he's moving forward.

"What are you guys up to today?" I ask.

Eva lifts Tam's hand. "Just looking at the windows. I used to work here."

I remember her telling me such a thing.

"And we're going to have tea in The Oak Room."

"Sounds fun." And expensive.

"We just came from the Christkindlmart," Eva adds.

I glance up as if the seasonal mart will magically appear. "Gosh, I can't remember the last time I went to that." Maybe in my twenties, pre-Mitch, pre-children. The German-themed fair, which sells authentic holiday décor and German inspired food is a city favorite and gathers quite a crowd.

"It's only three blocks away." Eva points in the general direction.

"I remember." An idea forms. "About that playdate? I'd love to get together. Maybe between Christmas and the New Year." I just need to get through the first holiday.

"Sounds perfect."

"Enjoy your tea."

"We will. And tell Nick I said hi."

The comment brings me up short. Why would she think I speak to Nick often? It was only a date. Maybe not even one. We simply attended a party together.

Or was it more?

I weakly smile in response and call Nash's attention.

To my surprise, Eva leans in and offers me a hug. "Merry Christmas, Holliday."

"Happy Holidays," I state, as I'd changed my language to the all-encompassing phrase while working at the bank.

Eva gives me a puzzled look at the monotone reply before stepping toward the door of the iconic department store.

"Who's hungry?" I ask the kids.

"McDonald's!" Nash shouts.

"Actually, I have something better in mind."

+ + +

The square set up with booths is only slightly less crowded mid-day compared to my memory, but I navigate the kids through the bustle of people to a hot dog vendor and then thankfully find a seat inside the beer and wine tent.

While enjoying a mulled hot wine, I watch Nash and Eloise animatedly tell me stories about kids in school. I'm laughing loudly when someone speaks beside me.

"That's a beautiful sound."

My head turns at the deep masculine voice. "Nick?"

"Hi, Nick," Nash excitedly speaks around a bite of hot dog.

"Hey, buddy," Nick addresses Nash.

"What are you doing here?" My voice is too high, too curious, and almost as excited as Nash's to finally see my neighbor.

Nick slips his hands into his jean pockets and sheepishly glances at me. "Just enjoying the festivities."

He no sooner says that when a gorgeous redhead slips her arm through his. "There you are."

I almost choke at how beautiful she is, all lean and tall with vibrant hair and a smattering of freckles on her face. Instantly, my stomach curdles my spiced wine.

"Holliday," Nick immediately says, watching my face morph to what I'm certain is envy on my cheeks. "This is my younger sister, Kaye." Nick slips his arm free of his sister, wraps it around her shoulders and then rubs his knuckles against her hair.

"Oh my God. You're such a child," she squeals pushing at his side before glancing at me. "Did he say Holliday? As in the hot neighbor?"

My eyes briefly close and I lower my head, shaking it side to side.

"What a liar you are, Nick," she admonishes. "You're freaking stunning."

Startled, I glance up, finding her eyes on me.

"I said she was hot."

Kaye snorts, shaking her head like men are stupid. "Hot implied a different sort of look. This . . ." She waves up and down at me. "Is gorgeous."

My face heats ten times before I finally find words. "Thank you. You're sweet."

Kaye turns to the kids. "And who are these two beauties?"

Nash and Eloise introduce themselves and Kaye engages them in conversation about Santa and what they asked for this Christmas.

Turning my attention to Nick, I ask, "Would you like to sit down?" I slide over on the bench seat, allowing space for him.

"I don't want to interrupt. Just saw you across the way and wanted to say hi. Then I heard you laugh. I haven't heard it often enough." His eyes dance while watching me, that ever-present gleam apparent, but dimmed the teeniest bit.

"Nick tells me you're writing a children's book," Kaye interjects on our locked eyes moment.

"Kaye," Nick groans, sheepishly looking at me once again, aware he's shared something private and personal with his sister.

"Oh. Well, it's just an idea." I brush off the dream and side-eye my children who are listening as little ears do.

"That's how anything starts," Kaye cheerfully responds. "But when you're ready to publish, reach out to me." She elbows her brother. "I have connections."

I'm reminded that Nick's family owns North Pole Toys. Kaye must work in the family business.

"Yeah, thank you. I'll think about it."

"Don't think. Do," Kaye says, then gives me a wink that must run in the family. She turns to her brother. "Now, I want a wiener schnitzel like Nash. Feed me."

"She said wiener," Nash giggles.

"She means a hot dog," Nick corrects, good-naturedly laughing at his sister. "You pain in the—" He stops short, glancing at the kids before insulting his sister.

"Nash. Eloise. Nice meeting you. I have it on good authority you've been very good this year." Kaye hitches her thumb at her brother. "Santa is proud. But your mom is prouder, remember that."

After a finger wave, she steps away but Nick lingers. "She's a nut this time of year."

"She's pretty. And sweet," I repeat about her compliments.

"She's right. I've had it wrong calling you hot, Holliday. You're beautiful." He leans down and kisses my head. "Be good for your mom," he says to the kids, then addresses all of us. "Merry Christmas."

As I watch him retreat, my insides are a clashing riot once again. He's talked to his sister about me. He thinks I'm beautiful.

And I miss him.

"She looked just like Kris Kringle's wife in that show," Eloise says, a little awe in her voice.

"What show?" I turn back to my daughter.

"*Santa Claus Is Coming to Town.*" The circa-1970 stop-motion Christmas program is a classic, and I glance back up to see Nick watching us from inside the entrance to the tent.

With a soft wave, he timidly smiles, aware he's been caught.

A thought hits me as I softly smile back and then return my attention to my children.

149

The greatest DO list I've been given is the two little people sitting opposite me. And while others might have expensive homes with fireplaces or access to a toy company, I have the best gift anyone could receive.

Incredible children.

They are that something more this season.

Chapter 13

Christmas Eve arrives, and we attend a children's mass in the early evening then head to my parents' house for dinner. The place is chaotic with my brother and his family present from Ohio.

By eight o'clock, we have the Santa tracker running on my phone and head home, searching the dark winter sky for a sleigh and eight reindeer. Pointing here and there toward the city sky, I keep up the charade despite the orange haze of streetlights reflected in the cloudy night. The threat of snow hangs in the air again and it'd be nice to have a white Christmas.

With a glance at Nick's dark house when I pull into my driveway, I ignore the tug in my chest, and hope he's with family this evening. Helping a groggy Nash into the house, Eloise follows, and soon enough they are tucked into their beds.

Santa isn't in the sky, but hard at work in living rooms everywhere, cursing instruction manuals and assembling objects. Maybe last-minute wrapping or simply arranging presents beneath a tree. With our stockings stuffed—I'd hung them on the short railing along my staircase—and the gifts underneath the evergreen, I take a quiet moment to enjoy the silence and the colorful lights of my tree. The live item is holding up well and I'm almost sad to take it down soon. Some people keep a fake tree up all year, decorating it in various themes according to the month or season. I'll never get to that kind of crazed enthusiasm.

Christmas is once a year, thankfully. But the magic of the season should be carried throughout the other three-hundred and sixty-four days of the calendar. Silently, I vow to do better next year. Come what may, I'll figure it out.

For some reason, I recall the window displays at Ashford's. The storyline felt a little lacking this year. While the annual effort was an attempt to draw in children, the plot is often for adults. The idea of a soldier dreaming of home for Christmas wasn't as poignant as it should have been.

I think about Eloise, who asked if we could return home, meaning our old house because of a silly fireplace.

Home. What does that word mean? What makes one?

Not the items within a place but the events and people that circulate around a person.

Suddenly, thoughts were racing, and I search for a notepad in the cluttered kitchen junk drawer. Seeking a pen, I only find the red marker I used to answer our elf's final questions. Tonight, he gets packed away for another year, with the understanding he's returned to the North Pole.

Please let my children still believe next year, I silently pray.

Then, I frantically write, plotting out an idea . . . for a children's book.

+ + +

Christmas morning, I contain the kids as long as I can. Their typically early-to-rise meter is turned up a notch or two and they both wake at five a.m. Needing a few more minutes as I'd spent half the night organizing and reorganizing my thoughts, I hold them off until six.

Then, I spring them loose.

Mitch was due at seven. He doesn't arrive until eight. When he starts to argue that I didn't wait, I hold up a hand to stop him. I'm not fighting with my ex on Christmas. I'd actually not like to speak to him as he never offered to pay for the Zlot 720 or the Like

Me Doll for Eloise. Mitch knows I'm under financial constraints again. He doesn't even blink with support. Of all the people I don't need in my life, Mitch is number one, but for the sake of our children I'm stuck with him for years.

He helps set up Nash's gaming system and nods once at Eloise's new doll.

I make breakfast which Mitch doesn't eat. He's eager to leave the house by ten.

"This didn't work," I say to him when the kids begrudgingly head upstairs to dress for the remainder of the day to be spent with Mitch's family. Nash is already a ball of exhaustion and whiny with tears because he wants to stay home and use his new games. Eloise asked if she could take her new doll with her and Mitch agreed, which led to Nash wanting to take the Zlot system with him. I refused.

Mitch isn't getting the honor of playing a game he didn't purchase with our son. Nor is the system going to mysteriously remain at his place.

"Yeah, we need to rethink next year." Mitch scratches the back of his neck, avoiding my eyes.

"Well, we have an entire year to reconsider." With a hand on the stairway banister, I take a step up on the landing preparing to check the kids have all the pieces of their outfits on. Socks. Underwear. (Yes, Nash can forget.)

"I'm asking Paige to marry me."

I brace for the stab to my chest. The saber sword to split me open. However, only a pinch hits my sternum, like a sudden case of heartburn.

I'm no longer in love with my ex. He destroyed that love. He isn't part of my life other than his role as the father of my children.

There's a man living next door with more concern for my kids than this guy, who is about to start a new family.

"Congratulations," I choke out. Not a drop of sincerity fills my voice, but I'm not envious of Paige. The twinge of disappointment is the idea Mitch has someone while I don't.

Then again, I have the kids and we'll be good. We have new traditions and a cute little house with a garage that tilts a little more to the left each day.

And a good neighbor who watches out for us, like the elf on the shelf, only Nick can't be packed in a shoe box. I don't want to bundle him up and store him away.

As I slowly climb the stairs, taking a second to calm my thoughts and blink away unwarranted tears, I consider that it might be time to write a new list for my future.

+ + +

When I called my parents to wish them a Merry Christmas, they asked me to join them for dinner, but I was feeling rather introspective and serene this year. I wanted the day to myself, especially after writing most of the night.

I'd planned to use the day to allow further inspiration to arise and decided to take a walk, hoping nature would speak to me. To the extent that one can find nature in a city. Snow had fallen overnight. The ground is covered in a light blanket of whiteness while the sidewalks and streets are free of any dusting.

The neighborhood is quiet. The local park is empty of children. A lone man quickly walks his dog, eager to return to his family or friends. As for me, I saunter, taking my time to breathe in the silence and fill my lungs with the fresh, cold air. The temperature is crisp and my cheeks chill, but I'm layered underneath my thick long coat and heavy boots.

I walk and I walk, and just take time, allowing my thoughts to scatter or collide.

And I think about my little story, evolving from an idea to a concept to a storyline about coming home for the holidays.

I am home. Inside my heart, I'm at peace. I'm happy with me, although the concern for a job prickles my thoughts.

Not today, I say.

I love my children. I love my parents. What more is there to need or do in life than the gift of love.

Eventually, with an ache in my legs and the cold filtering through the layers, I head toward my house. As I near, I notice Nick's truck in the shared driveway.

My heart does a strange little leap inside my chest, and I stumble over my own booted feet. I need to pass Nick's house to get to mine and I slow my gait, although I don't know what's suddenly weighing me down.

As I approach his place, his front door opens.

"Holliday," he quietly calls out.

"Merry Christmas, Nick." I stop on the sidewalk facing his house, hesitant while expectant. I should say something more. I should ask how he is. I should ask questions about his sister, his family. But all I can do is stare at the beautiful man who lives next door to me wearing dark jeans and a bright shirt, rolled to his elbows. The red cap rests on his head.

He steps out of his house, slipping on the leather jacket I've seen him wear before. Stalking up to me on the sidewalk, he stops a foot away, eyes inspecting me.

"Are you okay?" he asks, reminding me of how I asked him the same thing last summer.

Am I okay?

My smile is timid. "Yeah, I think I am," I admit, allowing my lips to curl higher. "How was your day?"

Nick shakes his head, still watching me. "How was yours?" He knows the kids went to Mitch's this afternoon.

"The kids were great this morning," I say, finding I mean every word. They were excited and thanking Santa, even though he wasn't present. *Wink-wink.* And just all around happy. "I fought with Mitch."

"Shit. What happened with Mitch?" Nick scratches his knuckles beneath his chin.

"He's proposing to Paige."

Nick continues to study me, assessing me. "How are you feeling about that?"

I turn my head, looking toward my house with its holiday lights twinkling in the twilight. "I feel strangely numb. Like I honestly don't care. It isn't about Mitch or Paige; it's the unfairness. That he's moving on and I'm . . ."

"What?" Nick steps closer, giving me a whiff of that bayberry and snow combination I've come to love. "What are you?"

Lonely. Stuck. Scared of the future.

Then I rethink. I have my children. I'm still young enough. And I'm a little excited about the *possibilities* of my unknown future.

"I'm just me, doing the best I can every day." I exhale, and a puff of white mist fills the space between us.

"And I think you're perfect every day."

"Nick," I sigh, lowering my head as my face heats.

"These last few days have been hell without you."

My head pops up and I take him in. His beard is a little thicker. His hair curls along the edge of his cap, suggesting it's longer, maybe in need of a cut. He looks tired, worn down a bit.

I tilt my head, needing answers. "You didn't call me all last week." After we slept together and baked cookies, I hadn't heard from him other than one short text until the afternoon I was fired.

He swipes at his hat, as if scratching an itch and then rights the cap again. With the beard and bright eyes, plus that shock of red on his head, he's a right-fucking-hot elf. But his looks will not detract me.

"I'm an idiot," he states before glancing away. "That night we had together." He turns back to face me. "It meant a lot to me."

I huff. He has a funny way of showing it.

As if reading my thoughts, he says, "I want to show you something." The request is strange, but his eyes are eager, almost desperate.

"Just give me five minutes of your time. Ten," he adds, hopeful, determined. "I can explain everything."

"Fine." My shoulders fall. I still don't have answers, but he points toward the driveway, and I walk up the lane. Nick places his hand on my lower back, clutching my coat to stop me from stepping up the stairs to his front door.

"It's out back." His voice is rusty, suddenly sounding uncertain about what he's going to show me. Then, he holds out his hand, reminding me of when he pulled me through the Botanic Garden, and I hesitantly take it.

When we round the corner of his house, I stop.

"You've been building a greenhouse." How very environmental of him, not to mention I'd love a greenhouse. The early plants I could grow. The start of vegetables. Nash and Eloise would love a garden. And all this from the woman who couldn't even cut her own grass last summer.

Nick tugs me forward and opens the door. As I step inside, he flips a switch and miniature lights come alive, speckling the walls and the ceiling like little stars, and reminding me of the tunnel we stood underneath the night he first kissed me.

"It's beautiful," I whisper about the empty space that's the size of a small room.

"I told you I needed to find a gift you couldn't shake and guess what's inside before you opened it."

Confused, I spin to face him. Suddenly, a fan hums to life and the room fills with tiny shreds of paper, like a slow exploding confetti gun.

Nick feeds the fan again, and more pieces dance around me.

"What is this?" I laugh as I look up at the paper floating about, lifting my hands, and watching bits fall against my palms, realizing the slivers aren't shreds but miniature paper snowflakes.

"The night we stood on the patio at the fundraiser, you mentioned a snow globe and freezing time. I'm not quite that powerful, Holliday. But I'd like my time to be spent with you."

My head lowers and I watch him through the shower fluttering inside the greenhouse.

"You got the wrong idea about that list and I'm sorry you misunderstood. You are *not* a project to me." Nick pauses then tilts his head. "Or maybe you are. There's something between us and I want to build and nurture it. I want it to grow."

He sets another clump of mini snowflakes in his hand free before the fan and steps up to me, cupping the sides of my face.

My heart clangs in my chest like ringing Christmas bells.

"I'm sorry you didn't hear from me last week. I worked and then took on an extra shift so I could have a day free when your kids were home. But I should have called. I should have explained myself. I just didn't want to rush you or pressure you or . . ." He huffs and tilts back his head. "I'm not good at speaking the emotional stuff."

"I think you're doing okay." I mean, he built me a snow globe. He's *doing* something to show me how he feels. His love language was clearly giving gifts and doing service.

His head instantly lowers. "I want us to be an *us*."

My eyes widened, surprised by the sudden directness. Thrilled a little, too. "I'm complicated, Nick. A package deal with Eloise and Nash."

"I know, and I like that even more." His thumbs stroke my cheeks. "Your kids are great. That's because of you, what you are building with them in your new home. And I just want a sliver of that newness, that fresh start."

I recall him telling me that all he'd done for me might not be about me.

"I don't even cut my own grass or shovel my drive."

"That's what I'm here for." He leans forward rubbing his surprisingly warm nose against mine.

"Is that all you're here for, though?" To help me out.

His thumbs slip beneath my chin and tip up my head, forcing me to meet his gaze. "No, honey. I'm here because I need you. And I want to be there for you, however you'll have me."

"I don't have a fireplace," I whisper, still arguing against us being together when being with him is really all I want.

He chuckles. "We'll work that out. *We. Us. Together.*"

"I'm unemployed, Nick." I drop my gaze from his face. Embarrassed. Disappointed in myself.

But Nick refuses to let me look away. His thumbs prompt my chin up again. "And you'll find a new job. A better one. One that suits you."

Eyes meeting his, I say, "You make it sound so simple."

"It can be. Believe, Holliday. Not just in this season, but all the year through. Believe in good things for yourself. You're a good person and you deserve the best."

He stares at me like he wants to imprint the thoughts into my head. I deserve what I want, and I want him.

I lick my lips. "Can I show *you* something? It's at my house."

His mouth quirks up at the corner, his brow arching to match. His voice drops. "I'd love to see it."

Seduction fills his face and I laugh to myself. While I wouldn't mind a repeat of our night by his fireplace together, what I have to show him isn't that.

I hope he isn't disappointed.

Chapter 14

Nick follows me to my house, and I take his coat, hanging it up in my front closet.

"I'll just be a minute. It's upstairs."

Nick watches me as I turn toward the staircase and race upward, my heart hammers with every step I climb.

Once in my room, I quickly find the notebook and turn, startled by Nick standing on the threshold of my bedroom.

"I . . . um . . . This is what I wanted to show you."

Holding the notebook between us, Nick's eyes meet mine, questioning me a second before he takes the bound pages from my hand. He flips the first page and then the second. Glancing back up at me, the sparkle I've come to adore in his eyes flares. He crosses the room and sits on the edge of my bed, taking his time, turning each page, examining every sheet.

"Holliday," he whispers. "Is this what I think it is?"

"It's just some ideas," I sheepishly admit, standing before him.

He places his palm reverently over the final page and looks up at me. "This is more than an idea. This is a story. A beautiful story about home and the holidays."

The story includes a list of things the little boy must do to get home for Christmas.

"Thank you," I whisper. "If you hadn't given me the nudge I needed, I might not have given this a second thought." I nod at the notebook. "Thank you for inspiring me."

Slowly, Nick's expression shifts, and he sets the notebook aside. He watches me as he speaks. "You're the inspiration, honey. You've been all the things on that list *to me*. That's why the items were checked off on my phone. Not because I'd completed something but because we'd done those things together."

"Nick," I whisper, cupping his jaw.

"My feelings for you started when you asked me last summer if I was okay. That day after Monica made a scene in my yard. You asked about me. Not what happened. Not who she was. *Me*." Nick points at himself. "You gave me grace."

He stares at me. "Then I mowed your lawn and you put a flowerpot on my front stoop."

"It was nothing in comparison," I softly laugh.

"But you did something for me. You showed me how you were thankful, generous, considerate. It was nice. It made me feel good. Made the outside of my place look like a home, not just a house."

His hands come to my hips, and he jostles me. "You're a good person, Holliday. And that's a gift."

I timidly chuckle. He's the good person. "You know I only wanted to be a little bad."

He chuckles, rich and deep. "Oh, you've made that list, too. There's a sub list to the set list which puts you in the good person, but occasionally naughty, column."

"Just occasionally," I tease.

Nick slowly stands and cups my face. "I'd like it to be more often. I'm thinking every night." He kisses me, soft and sweet, tasting of peppermint and promises.

"What are you suggesting?" Friends with benefits. Naughty next-door neighbors.

"Build a life with me."

"Nick," I whisper, my shoulders relaxing. My insides rioting. This is so much more than I expected.

"I bet you wrote another list, and on it you put buy a gift for Nick."

"How did you know that?" I laugh, envisioning the sticky note I'd written, although I didn't need the reminder.

"I'd like to amend that list." Nick leans forward and rubs his nose against mine. "Let's just have love Nick on the list."

My head pulls back, and I meet his eyes. "I do. Love you, that is." I'm shocked while confident in what I've said. "I love you."

Nick's smile is the largest I've ever seen. White teeth. Gleaming eyes. "And I love you right back, honey."

His mouth is suddenly on mine, kissing me long and sweet before shifting to heated and spicy.

"I want to wrap you up and then unwrap you. You'll be my personal Christmas present."

I hum against his mouth, eager to keep kissing him. "How does that work?"

Nick pauses our kissing fest and catches my gaze. "Undress. Slowly." He lowers to the edge of my bed, watching me, waiting on me.

I have layers and layers to peel, from my sweater to my long underwear. The striptease isn't nearly as seductive as he might have hoped as I stumble a few times to tug tight clothing free and I giggle at my clumsiness.

All the while, Nick sits on my bed, a jovial crook on his mouth as he watches me reveal myself. When I'm naked, skin pebbling from both the coolness of the room and the heat in his gaze, Nick pulls a long spool of ribbon from his back pocket.

"Where did that come from?"

"Magic." He winks as it unrolls, and he stands. "Now, I'm going to wrap you up."

But I thought— My thoughts scatter as he takes the silky ribbon and runs it along my neck and down my breast, brushing ever so lightly over my nipple, causing the sharp peak to harden even more. My breasts ache, heavy and eager for further attention, but Nick takes his time, running that ribbon over my skin. Along my shoulder and down my arm. Across my waist and up my middle.

"Ready to be naughty, snow lady."

I shiver at the cool tone of his voice and the hotness of his intentions. "Yes."

"Turn around."

I do as he says, and he starts by wrapping the ribbon around my waist, then slowly, intricately, crisscrossing beneath my breasts, trussing up the achy swells, before rounding my neck. He pulls my arms together, pinning my wrists behind me. The ribbon is soft while securing. I'm completely at his mercy.

Next, he surrounds my legs, wrapping them loosely in a downward swirl until my ankles are bound together. I can't step forward. I can't lean back. I'm completely immobile.

"You're doing so good, naughty girl," Nick mutters behind me once he stands, and I shiver underneath his praise. With an arm around my waist, he spins me around and lowers my upper half for the bed. With my cheek pressed to the mattress, I watch him tug off his shirt and notice his socks are already gone. He hastily unbuckles his belt and tugs it free from his jeans. The sharp snap of leather causes me to flinch.

He drops the belt with a heavy clunk on the hardwood floor. Then he's popping open the button on his pants and lowering his zipper, revealing his straining length.

Nick drops to his knees behind me, fondling the globes of my backside. "I'm going to lick you like the giant candy cane you are."

The first swipe of his tongue has me shooting forward a bit and preening at the delicious heat. With the red ribbon tying me together, I might look like a peppermint stick. One desperate to be eaten.

Nick doesn't disappoint. With his mouth on me, in a position I've never explored, I'm quick to be sticky and sweet from his attention, groaning and begging for every lick. Near the edge, Nick retreats and I cry out, frantic to reach for him. Only I can't move. With my arms pinned behind me and my body bent in half, I'm at his mercy.

"Jesus, you look amazing like this." His voice is smoky and rough as he lowers his jeans and briefs.

I cry out again as the heat of his tip is dragged through swollen folds.

He's invented the naughty list.

He's made the top.

And he's proud of his position of torture.

Then I hear the rip of a packet and I struggle to watch over my shoulder as he covers himself.

Quickly, he's at my entrance, his tip kissing folds eager to open for him, to take him into me. "Have you been good or bad this year, Holliday?"

"Bad," I mumble toward the mattress. "So, so bad."

"Did Santa bring you a lump of coal?" he teases me, sliding the crown against my clit, teasing me.

"No," I groan.

Nick freezes.

"He brought me you."

"Holliday," he moans before he glides into me, drawing out the pleasure until he's to the hilt. "Am I what you wished for this year? Did you ask Santa for me?"

"I did," I moan as he pulls back then rushes forward. "I wanted you naked under my tree."

Nick chuckles, running his hand along the ribbon tied around my body. With my legs tightly wrapped, he easily slides in and out, hitting a place deep within me.

"Over a week ago, I had you underneath *my* tree, but that's semantics. And over a week is too long, honey."

In and out he moves, igniting the passion between us higher and higher. My body rocks as best it can to meet his thrusts but staying still almost has its advantages as well. Nick works me until I'm a sappy mess, then I crack and break, crumbling from the intensity. I'm dissolving beneath him, melting like a savory treat on the tongue.

Nick picks up the pace, surging into me. His fingers dig into my hips. Then, he's lifting me by the ribbons at my wrist. I cry out at the shift, sparked once again by something deep inside me.

"Nick?" The question is a plea. I don't seem to understand my own body.

His arms wrap around me. His fingers seek my clit. He's working me like a masterful puppeteer until I'm ready to unravel again.

"Nick!" I'm completely under his control and willingly following his lead.

"You're such a good girl," he murmurs behind me, praise fills his tone while salacious and scandalous at the same time. Additional words about taking him deep and him filling me up flitter through my head until I'm blissed out and blustering beneath him again. My body goes stiff before my knees give out.

Nick lowers me back to the bed and thrusts one final time before moaning in relief. "Holliday."

My name is more than this moment.

As he collapses over me, his breath is heavy at my ear. "Happy, Holliday." The phrase is more of a question.

"I'm happier than I've been in a long time." Tears prickle behind my eyes. I don't want this night to end. I don't want this season to be over. I don't want him to leave my bed.

"That's what I asked of Santa. To make you happy, Holliday."

"Nick," I whisper as he shifts to my side. "Why?"

"There's just something magical about you." He reaches for my hair, sweaty and loose around my face and brushes it behind my ear.

"There's something special about you, too." Comfort and joy. Patience and peace.

Nick leans in to kiss me quick before pulling back. "I'm going to unwrap you now." His eyes twinkle with mischief. The unwrapping of a gift is typically the exciting part but being wrapped up has been amazing.

Nick peppers me with kisses as he releases my ankles first and unwinds the ribbon up my legs. He kisses the backs of my knees and my outer thighs. I hiss as he drags the thin, slinky material across sensitive folds before untying my waist. My wrists are freed, and I roll them as Nick unbinds my lower arms. I slip to my knees at the edge of the bed while he slowly peels the ribbon from around my neck and under my breasts, until all my flesh and parts are unbound. Standing behind me, he tips my head back and cups my jaw.

"How about a bath, honey?"

I nod, unable to speak, and probably unable to move as I'd just had the most incredible moment of my life.

Nick scoops me up and carries me to the tub.

And in the warmth of a bubble bath, I marvel at how it's turned out to be a wonderful Christmas and a very good night.

Epilogue

The fifth day of Christmas . . .

[Nick]

When Holliday moved in next door, it was like an angel had been sent down from heaven to torture me. That hair. Those curves. Her eyes. I'd caught her a time or two watching me. Not inspecting me. Not questioning who I was or what I'd become, but just looking at me.

My former neighbor, Pete, was a hilarious old guy, and he warned me he'd sold the house to a single mom with two kids. *Warning* meaning I was to behave myself with my new neighbor. Look out for her, he'd said, but don't do her. The man was a horndog into his nineties.

I had nothing against pursuing a single mother. They were typically some of the strongest women I knew. Stubborn, too, as Holliday proved to be the first time I mowed her grass. *Buy yourself something pretty*, she'd said. Pure honey in that firecracker sarcasm. My dick was instantly hard.

But I fell for her before that moment. When she asked me if I was okay after the fight with Monica. Not what happened. Not who that woman was. Holliday asked about *me*.

Monica had actually been the fourth woman I'd tried to date with consistency because everyone was telling me I was getting older. I needed to settle down. I needed to find someone. However, the right woman had been hard to find. One who wouldn't take advantage of me. Wonder who I'd been. Where I came from. I had trouble trusting people.

That didn't mean I don't believe in the common good in people. Doing good deeds for others is who I am, how I'm built. I never expect anything in return. So that first time I cut Holliday's grass and she put a flowerpot on my stoop, I was stumped.

I can't say I purposefully planned every next action afterward, but for every action I did for her, she gave something back to me. Like she was silently grateful. Never making a big deal about anything but still appreciative.

And I fell harder, becoming a little addicted to this dance we did, where I felt like she needed me, but it was even more. She was thankful for me being next door.

I'd learned bits and pieces about her over the months. Nash and Eloise were sweet and not always silent about their mom. She didn't drink coffee. She worked long hours at a bank. She fought with her ex.

I hated her being alone, but I'd seen her fiery spirit. Felt it, too, with the fight we had days before Christmas.

Now we were on the fifth day of Christmas, and she'd been showing me over and over again how fun she could be and how she felt about me.

That Christmas night after I tied her up, and made mad love to her wrapped in ribbon, she came back to her bed, after claiming she needed a drink of water, with a pear in her hand.

"What's this?" I'd chuckled.

"It's a pear. And it's the first day of Christmas. I don't have a pear tree. And this might be recycled from the fruit basket the bank sent as an unimaginative gift for the holidays but—"

I hadn't let her finish, yanking the pear out of her hand, taking a big bite and then kissing her with my sticky lips. She'd been turning pink with her explanation as if slowly shutting down, embarrassed by how cute, thoughtful, and creative her gesture was on the first true day of Christmas. I loved that as a woman struggling with Christmas, she still had an affinity for the season.

I'd taken that half-eaten pear and rubbed it on parts of her I could lap up, and the rest of the night had been a dream.

As the next day returned her children from her douchy ex, and I had the day off, I played up the second day of Christmas to prove I was all-in with the package deal Holliday claimed she was with the kids. She was a gift. A built-in family and I wanted them. So, while I didn't think Holliday would appreciate two turtle doves, I gave Nash and Eloise each a turtle instead. Nash named his Rock; Eloise named hers Snowflake. Her first question to her shelf elf next year might be: Does he like turtles?

Since I had to work the following day, I sent three French takeout dinners, so Holliday didn't have to cook. She saved me the Napoleon bar dessert and we ate it together after my shift, when the kids were in bed. Then, we made out on her couch for a while.

On the fourth day, I had to work again, but I called her four times. Not a text. An actual call. By the fourth random one where I asked her if she had a favorite bird, she was onto me.

"Are you giving me four calling birds?"

"Nope, just four phone calls to tell you I'm thinking of you."

"I'm thinking of you, too." Her voice softened. I could almost see her cheeks pinkening. I wanted to see her entire body glowing again.

By the fifth day of Christmas, because yes, they actually occur after December 24th, I had something special in mind.

"Is that an extra present in your tree?"

"Where?" Holliday says leaning forward from our seat snuggled on her couch, admiring her tree one final time. Tomorrow morning she plans to take it down so she has a clean house for the new year, when traditionally Christmas trees should remain up until the twelve days of the Christmas season are complete.

Holliday squints at the softly-lit evergreen in her otherwise dark living room.

"Right there, between the karate ornament and a snowman made from marshmallows."

Holliday turns her head toward me. "What did you do?" She whispers but a smile curls her lush mouth. One I plan to be kissing on this couch in a few minutes.

"Wasn't me. Must have been that elf."

Holliday rolls her eyes and laughs. That pesky holiday doll left her a new DO list on her refrigerator.

Build life together.

Love Nick forever.

Be happy and better.

Not that anything about Holliday needs improving. I just want a better year ahead for her.

"Nick," she soft groans in a way I love. When I know she *is* happy. She slips off the couch and returns with the small box.

Her hand trembles and I'm a little anxious myself. I feel like I should warn her, give her an explanation before she opens the gift, but she's quick to pop the hinged lid.

A light laugh fills her throat, and her smile grows brighter. "Five gold stacking rings."

The thin rings include three simple bands, one with a heart and one with an evergreen.

"So you'll look at them and remember me."

Her head pops upward, her eyes soften. "You're unforgettable," she speaks quietly before kissing me, sucking at my mouth like she can't get enough.

Then she pulls back. "And unbelievable. This has to stop. I'm afraid six geese are going to be in my yard tomorrow." She laughs. "And what will you do for ten lords a leaping? It's too much. Stop," she laughs harder, louder.

"Shh. The kids." I press a finger against her lips. "I got it all planned, honey."

"It's too much."

"Let me do this for you." With my eyes focused on hers, she grins, accepting I want to do these things. Not because she's a project. Or I'm ticking down a list. "I love this holiday. And I love you."

"I love you, too," she says before fitting the stacking rings onto her finger and snapping the box shut. Holding out her hand to inspect the glittery jewelry, she says, "Those six geese were a layin'. Think we could amend it to getting laid?"

Strong, sharp laughter leaves my throat as I tackle her down to the couch.

"Holliday," I groan before capturing her mouth.

She's my favorite season.

For twelve days, and all the other days of the year.

I believe in her.

And she believes in me.

Thank you for taking the time to read this book.
Please consider writing a review on major sales channels where ebooks and paperbacks are sold and discussed.

Want the remainder of the twelve days of Christmas from Nick's perspective?

Naughty-ish Bonus

If you enjoy a SHE-grump during the holidays,
you'll also love Eva and Zebb's story in *Scrooge-ish*.

Flip the page for an excerpt.

Love silver foxes in your romance reads?
You might enjoy *Sterling Heat*.
Where the curmudgeon baker delivers a baby in his bakery and falls for the single mother.

L.B. DUNBAR

THE LIST

~~See the lights~~. Be the light.

~~Buy presents~~. Be present.

~~Wrap gifts~~. Wrap someone in a hug.

~~Send gifts~~. Send peace.

~~Shop for food~~. Donate food (and time).

~~Make cookies~~. Make love.

Additional items:

Build a home (full of traditions).

Love your family.

Be happy and better.

Sample *Scrooge-ish*

THE REUNION

1

I hate Christmas.

I don't know who thought every female must love shopping, wrapping, baking and hosting—as commercialized on nearly every holiday advertisement—but if those things are supposed to be coded into my DNA, I'm missing it.

And my hatred is exacerbated each year by gifts given more from obligation than love, well wishes without heart behind them, and family.

Don't get me wrong. I know Christmas isn't about gifts. The season wasn't born in a store, and I believe that kindness can be found in a word or smile just as much as a deed, but something is always missing for me.

Somewhere along the way, I stopped caring about this holiday.

Maybe it was when certain people stopped caring about me.

Refer back to reference three above: Family.

What's the worst is I work in retail, where the happiest time of the year is accentuated by the beep-beep of chip scanners, the screaming emotional meltdown of children, and annoying, selfish customers. I'm in management at Ashford's, a top-end department store in downtown Chicago, open seven days a week because my boss is an asshole.

I work a lot of hours, volunteering to fill in for others because they have families, or family emergencies, or friends with families who have emergencies, and more work for me means more money toward my dream. It also means less time facing reality.

I don't have a life.

And I'm lonely.

But no worries. It's late Wednesday, Thanksgiving Eve, which has somehow become a thing on the night before an American holiday, and I'm working.

"What are you still doing here?" Zaleya asks me as I hand over two bulging bags of random clothes to some older woman who has no idea what she's just purchased for her grandchildren. Cha-ching, cha-ching, though...

"I'm working."

"But you were off at six and now it's eight." Zaleya Stone is a curvy brunette with a huge heart and an infectious smile. She's excellent with difficult customers and a dream to work with.

"Eight. Six. They both have a little, swirly circle at the bottom of them." I shrug giving Zaleya a smile. The Ashford's smile. The I'm-happy-to-work-here-even-though-I'm-really-miserable-but-need-the-money smile.

"Ev-a," Zaleya draws out my name. At least she says it correctly. Ev-ah, like Evan without an -n. Not Eve-ah, or even Evie, or Eve, or whatever name Jude Ashford likes to say when he grows frustrated in a management meeting and can't remember my name despite eight years working here and making top manager three years in a row. Jude is younger than me and the owner of the entire company. He's also hot which makes him even more annoying, but I'm not into the cougar-thing.

"You have a thing tonight," Zaleya reminds me although I really don't want the reminder. I mean, who celebrates twenty-two years since high school graduation? We were supposed to have a twentieth in 2020, when a world pandemic hit, and the celebration had to be cancelled. Then the alumni organization wanted to host a glorious twenty-one the following year, only the planning committee members contracted COVID from each other. Gossip on the street, though, is the cancellation was because a set of former high school sweethearts and two former jocks leading the planning had a four-way one weekend that ended a marriage and a business partnership. It was a scandalous situation the high school couldn't allow affiliated with the reputation and prestige of good old Immaculate Academy.

"Oh, I'm not going." I force another smile as I nod at the next customer to step forward. I shouldn't be working a register, but the floor is busy despite being the night before Thanksgiving. We're running a door-buster deal this evening as a jumpstart on Black Friday's five a.m. opening time. We used to open late night on Thanksgiving, but we've canceled that extra evening of potential revenue. To be closed on a national holiday actually felt rather compassionate which wasn't my thing.

I've been told I'm selfish and unfeeling, according to my last three attempts at relationships. And while I tend to agree with that assessment, I stopped caring a long time ago.

"You have to go," Zaleya admonishes me.

"I don't have to do anything." I ring up a female customer's purchase, hoping she isn't intending to wear the two items purchased in combination.

Zaleya nudges me out of the way before the next customer steps forward, swipes her team member card through the register, and logs me off the system. Somehow, she's overridden the program and clocks me out of work.

"I could write you up for insubordination and unethical practices." I narrow my eyes at her, without any heat in my threat. Zaleya is older than me by almost two decades, but under me as an assistant manager.

"One day that veneer is going to slip, and you'll realize a real softy lives beneath that tight leather skirt and take no prisoners heels." Zaleya winks.

"Don't you mean others will realize . . . and also, you're wrong. Nothing soft here." I pat my belly, which actually does jiggle a little and grumbles, reminding me I haven't eaten all day.

"Yeah, well, eat some peppermint bark or a Christmas cookie . . . or five. And put some roast beast on those bones." She eyes me up and down, and I marvel at her use of a Grinch reference.

I like Zaleya. She reminds me of the mother I never had, which doesn't make sense as my mother is still around. Can't have a memory of someone who didn't exist, though. Mom left on Christmas Eve, when I was ten, and Dad cancelled the holiday that year. And most years after that. Zaleya is more like a mentor, or a guardian angel, if I believed in such a thing. She's just an overall nice person, and I hate her a little for her good cheer. But not really.

Zaleya nudges me out of the register station. "Get going. I predict great things from this evening."

+ + +

By eight-thirty, Zaleya catches me still lingering in my meager office on the upper floors of Ashford's. The flagship store is the last remaining Ashford's. The company was bought out, and all but the landmark location was converted to the other conglomerate's brand. Gossip around the water cooler, so to speak, is that Jude inherited the single store, instead of the brand going to his father. As the sole family member who owns Ashford's, I've heard words like spoiled, entitled, and ungrateful for his inheritance used to reference him. On a side note, we don't have water coolers because Jude is too cheap to pay for such a service for his employees.

"Eva." Zaleya's motherly tone is both admonishing and chagrin.

"It's too late to go."

"It's only eight-thirty. You young things are just getting started at this hour."

I'm no longer young. I'll be turning forty this December.

"I'm not dressed."

Zaleya eyes my outfit, taking in the leather pencil skirt in bright red I'm wearing. I'd worn it in an effort to appear holiday-cheery when I'm not.

"You look gorgeous."

"I'm too old to attend these things. I mean, who goes to high school reunions, really? Jocks who can't let go of state championships two decades-old and still wear their high school rings. Nerds who want to show everyone they made it financially. The pimply kid who wants to prove he was a supermodel underneath his skin. The homecoming queen who popped out three kids before thirty and is divorced from her second husband."

Zaleya stares at me.

"Where does that put me?" Not jock. Not geek. Just your average girl in high school. Good grades, clean-cut, and boring.

"It puts you attending. Not to prove anything to them but to allow yourself a night out on the town among people you once knew."

"But that's my point. I don't know these people anymore. I hardly knew them twenty-two years ago."

"Just go. 'Tis the season." Zaleya waves a hand above her head. "Magic is in the air."

"The season doesn't officially begin until tomorrow, when Santa drives his sleigh before Ashford's in the parade." Sarcasm fills my voice. I don't believe in Santa any more than I believe in magic.

Zaleya puts her hands on her hips. "Honey, Christmas lives all the year through."

Jiminy Cricket, she sounds like a holiday card.

"Who knows? Maybe an old boyfriend will be there." Zaleya wiggles her brows.

I snort.

"Or a boy of former interest." Her voice hitches, gushing with innuendo.

I huff.

But someone does come to mind.

Someone I deny myself the chance to remember, as I'm certain he's forgotten me.

Learn how Eva's reunion goes by reading *Scrooge-ish*.

More by L.B. Dunbar

Sterling Falls

Small town. Big heart. Seven siblings muddling their way through love over 40.

Sterling Heat
Sterling Brick
Sterling Streak

Parentmoon

When the mother of the groom goes head-to-head with the single father of the bride.

Holiday Hotties (Christmas novellas)

Holiday novellas certain to heat the season.

Scrooge-ish
Naughty-ish

Road Trips & Romance

3 sisters. 3 destinations. A second chance at love over 40.

Hauling Ashe
Merging Wright
Rhode Trip

Lakeside Cottage

Four friends. Four summers. Shenanigans and love happen at the lake.

Living at 40
Loving at 40
Learning at 40
Letting Go at 40

The Silver Foxes of Blue Ridge

Small mountain town, silver foxes. Brothers seeking love over 40.

Silver Brewer
Silver Player
Silver Mayor
Silver Biker

Sexy Silver Foxes

NAUGHTY-ish

When sexy silver foxes meet the feisty vixens of their dreams.
After Care
Midlife Crisis
Restored Dreams
Second Chance
Wine&Dine

Collision novellas
A spin-off from After Care – the younger set/rock stars
Collide
Caught

Rom-com standalone for the over 40
The Sex Education of M.E.

The Heart Collection
Small town, big hearts - stories of family and love.
Speak from the Heart
Read with your Heart
Look with your Heart
Fight from the Heart
View with your Heart

A Heart Collection Spin-off
The Heart Remembers

BOOKS IN OTHER AUTHOR WORLDS
Smartypants Romance (an imprint of Penny Reid)
Tales of the Winters sisters set in Green Valley.
Love in Due Time
Love in Deed
Love in a Pickle

The World of True North (an imprint of Sarina Bowen)
Welcome to Vermont! And the Busy Bean Café.
Cowboy
Studfinder

THE EARLY YEARS
The Legendary Rock Star Series
A classic tale with a modern twist of rock star romance and suspense
The Legend of Arturo King
The Story of Lansing Lotte
The Quest of Perkins Vale
The Truth of Tristan Lyons
The Trials of Guinevere DeGrance

Paradise Stories
MMA romance. Two brothers. One fight.
Abel
Cain

The Island Duet
Intrigue and suspense. The island knows what you've done.
Redemption Island
Return to the Island

Modern Descendants – writing as elda lore
Magical realism. Modern myths of Greek gods.
Hades
Solis
Heph

About the Author
www.lbdunbar.com

L.B. Dunbar loves sexy silver foxes, second chances, and small towns. If you enjoy older characters in your romance reads, including a hero with a little silver in his scruff and a heroine rediscovering her worth, then welcome to romance for those over 40. L.B. Dunbar's signature works include women and men in their prime taking another turn at love and happily ever after. She's a *USA TODAY* Bestseller as well as #1 Bestseller on Amazon in Later in Life Romance with her Lakeside Cottage and Road Trips & Romance series. L.B. lives in Chicago with her own sexy silver fox.

To get all the scoop about the self-proclaimed queen of silver fox romance, join her on Facebook at Loving L.B. or receive her monthly newsletter, Love Notes.

+ + +

Connect with L.B. Dunbar

Printed in the USA
CPSIA information can be obtained
at www.ICGtesting.com
LVHW080505031223
765364LV00015B/1083

9 781956 337358